outer-space adventures inspired by pulp fiction of the
1950's & 1960's conjured by
Rylan John Cavell

Thanks to David Richards

THE VENUMAN
FLY TRAP
AND OTHER STORIES

Petunia

Crazy Mal's Used Car Lot

The Red Wind

Stardust And Diamond

The Venusian Fly Trap

Farewell Tour

Something Else

The Deep

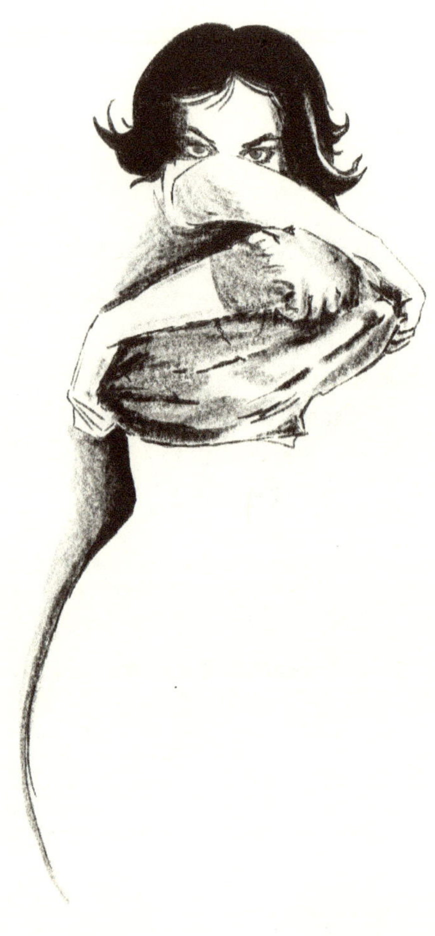

Petunia

"I'm paying for sex and dinner." Ade said, handing over the brown envelope of cash.

"In that order?" The woman asked, pausing to rifle her orange painted fingernails through the notes. Satisfied, she pushed the envelope into her cleavage.

He took her arm, and guided her across the shady street, to the front door of a mid-range restaurant.

"I was hoping for somewhere swankier." She said, "My other clients know how to treat a lady."

Ade held the door open, and ignored her jibe, "I like this place." He said, following her inside, "They do good breadsticks."

*

"What's your name?" Ade asked, as they perused the menu. He had forgotten what it had said under her photo in the catalogue, and had no qualms about admitting that.

"Petunia. Pet to my friends."

"Pet. Nice."

"Petunia. We're not friends."

Ade shrugged, and thanked the waiter as their drinks order arrived. A pint of lager for him, a glass of champagne for her. The waiter nodded, then drifted away, his servos whirring quietly.

"I can recommend the fish." Ade said.

Petunia sniffed her little nose distastefully, "Don't be ordering fish if you expect me to kiss you later. You're not paying me enough to put up with the whiff of hot seafood on your breath."

Ade was beginning to regret his choice of companion for the evening. But he had paid his money. He knew the deal; no refunds. So he may as well try and get his money's worth.

"So what's a pretty girl like you doing in a grim place like this?" He asked, deciding on his choice of dish and laying down the menu.

"Really?" She cocked a razor-thin eyebrow, "you're using that old line?"

"It's a way to start a conversation."

"I came here for the scenery." Petunia said, sipping her champagne.

Ade sighed at her sarcastic reply. Circumference City was grey, bland, and bleak. There was no scenery. The planet's rotation ensured one side always pointed at the sun, the other out to the darkness of space, so depending on whether you preferred a more

Mediterranean or Scandinavian ambience, you had a choice of Sun-side or Shade-side of the singular street that made up the 'city'; One street, that ran uninterrupted around the planet.

The restaurant was Sun-side, so from the conservatory at the rear of the building, it was constant, blazing midsummer. Ade's apartment, on the other hand, was Shade-side, and snow and ice regularly covered his midnight window.

Ade pulled at his shirt collar. He always found the Sun-side buildings a little too humid. But he enjoyed the food at this restaurant, so would put up with the discomfort.

"Been here long?" He asked, attempting more conversation.

"Are you ready to order?" Petunia asked, waving over one of the waiters.

Ade placed his order, "Olives and breadsticks for starters, then the carbonara, with garlic bread."

"Forget the garlic bread." Petunia said, wrinkling her nose to indicate yet another smell she was not being paid enough to spend the evening with.

"Ok, forget the garlic bread." Ade said reluctantly.

"Madame?" The waiter turned to Petunia.

"The soup to start, and a light salad for my main. Something with sun-blushed tomatoes. And keep me topped up." She waved her champagne glass at the waiter, who nodded and whizzed away.

The restaurant buzzed with conversation, the clink of glasses and cutlery, and the whirr of mechanical waiting staff. This gentle hubbub was relaxing, and Ade imagined he was back home on Earth, on the southern coast of France or Spain. Anywhere but this distant, ignored, decaying outpost of Human civilisation.

Petunia fidgeted, pulling from her handbag a cigarette case. She extracted a long purple Vogue and lit it with the candle that sat on their table. She sucked the grey fumes in deeply, then sat staring at Ade. When she spoke, each syllable emerged like smoke signals.

"I was born here." She said.

"Sorry?"

"You asked me if I'd been here long. I was born here. It's all I've known."

"I'm sorry."

"Don't be."

Ade gulped at his pint, wiping his wet lips on the back of his sleeve, "I grew up on Earth, in Europe. Fancied making my fortune with the Banking relocation of the early 50's."

Petunia nodded, taking another long, deep drag on her strange purple cigarette. It smelled of liquorice. Adjusting her top to better showcase her cleavage, Petunia tapped ash onto the floor, "Let me guess?"

"Guess what?"

She waved the smouldering stick at Ade to indicate she meant to fathom him out. Sitting back, she crossed one arm across her chest, stroking herself as she thought, "You moved to this rock with the family, like everyone else, chasing the money and hoping to make a fortune. You had a wife and two kids. They followed your dreams, but it all went pear-shaped. The money dried up. Started owing more than you were making. Mama flew home with the little money she could squeeze from the divorce settlement, taking the kids with her, leaving you here in a cheap flat and a dead-end job. No friends, no prospects, and nowhere near enough cash to charter passage home. And even if you did, who would have you? Where would you go? Years languishing on Mercury can't have done any favours for your curriculum vitae. So here you are; Trapped. And spending what little disposable income you have on evenings with girls like me. Am I close?"

"Three."

"Three?"

"Three children. Not two. Agnes, Loreta and Ingrid."

"Awful names."

Ade didn't care for her tone, and scowled at her.

"Oh don't look at me like that." She sneered, "what's past is past. You have to look on the sunny side of life, else you'd languish in misery." She stubbed out her cigarette.

Their starters arrived, and Ade tucked into the crunchy, crumbly breadsticks, while Petunia sipped soup daintily from a spoon.

"So how dirty a fuck am I providing for you tonight?" Petunia asked, not looking up.

Ade wheezed a spray of crumbs across the table, taken by surprise. He hadn't expected the topic of sex to come up until later, until they were in private! He hoped the family sat at the next table hadn't heard her.

"Let me enjoy the meal first." Ade said, choking, and wiping his mouth.

She laid her spoon down, and pushed away her bowl. She was finished, after only a couple of spoonfuls.

"Not hungry?"

"Saving myself for later." She grinned at him.

Ade picked off his olives one by one, skewering them with a plastic tooth pick. Petunia was unusual. She had a confidence other girls from Madam Mirage's catalogue lacked. They were meek, barely spoke, and were, well, less *brazen*. He supposed that Petunia must be a new addition to their roster, and therefore much less disillusioned with her situation. He had never met anyone quite like Petunia, with her bright nails, fancy cigarettes, and forthright manner. No one in Circumference City wore anything like her, or painted themselves with bright colours like her. It was what had attracted him to her picture in the first place.

"You were born here?" He asked.

She nodded, lighting another cigarette.

"Your parents still around?"

"Would it matter if they were?"

"Just making conversation."

"Mother is. Dad died before I was born."

"How did you come to work as... how did you come to do... the work you do?"

"How did I become a prostitute?"

"Keep your voice down!" Ade's eyes darted about, but the other patrons seemed engrossed in their own conversations, and ignorant of theirs.

"Relax." Petunia laughed at him, a little condescendingly, he thought, "I went into a line of work that pays well, and a job at which I excel. Simple enough."

Petunia had her glass refilled by one of the gently whirring waiting staff, and she stared at Ade as she sipped.

"What is it?" He asked.

"Nothing. Just wondering what you'll taste like." She ran her tongue over her lips.

Ade gulped, and felt the heat of embarrassment reddening his cheeks, "I, um, well..." She really was quite unlike anyone else.

"How old are you?" She asked.

"Fifty Two." He was grateful for the change in topic.

"Thought you were older." She said, almost unkindly, "but if you can still get it up, then we're all good, aren't we?"

"I assure you, I can." Ade said, lowering his voice.

Their mains arrived, and they ate in silence. Petunia ate a tiny mouthful, and was done, leaving her salad, as her soup, pretty much untouched.

"Adrian Cribbage, isn't it?" Said a booming voice across the gentle restaurant murmur.

Ade started, dropping his fork with a clatter. He stood up, stiff and alert, as a spherical man strode toward him, one arm had a rolled up newspaper tucked beneath it, the other was outstretched towards Ade. Ade took the offered hand, and shook it.

"Fancy seeing you here." The large man boomed, "Seen that the aliens have been making a pest of themselves again?" He said, indicating the paper in his armpit. Adrian hadn't, and didn't care much for galactic news. There was enough stress in his life, without the troubles of the galaxy causing him to fret further.

The round man's eyes, surveying the scene, alighted on Petunia. She was sucking on another purple cigarette, watching him with impassive eyes.

"Mr Ripe, this is..." Ade fumbled for words, unsure how to explain who or what Petunia was to him.

The large man loomed at her, bending forward, then took her hand and kissed it lightly, "I do hope we're still on for this weekend, Pet?" He said conspiratorially.

Petunia winked at him, and the man giggled like a schoolboy.

"Have a good night, Cribbage." The fat man slapped Ade on the shoulder with a meaty palm, "See you in the office tomorrow."

Ade sunk back into his chair, wiping sweat from his brow with a paper napkin, "You know my boss? You know Mr Ripe?" He asked.

Petunia smiled, "He's a regular. What his wife can't give him, and his secretary won't; I provide."

*

Through sporadic bouts of small talk, the evening progressed into night. The Mediterranean sun through the conservatory didn't move an inch.

"Do you want to see the sweet menu?" Ade asked, "They do a hearty spotted dick."

Petunia raises an eyebrow, and shook a hand to indicate she had eaten sufficiently, "Can we go back to yours now?" She packed her cigarette case away into her handbag, "or do you prefer al fresco fornication?"

Blushing, Ade paid for their meals. He downed the last mouthful of his lager, and escorted Petunia from the building. He hadn't appreciated before, how slight she was; A waspish waist, slender but pleasingly round hips, and angular shoulders. He pulled at his collar, feeling uncomfortable in his own heat, rather than the heat of the sun.

She linked arms with him, and allowed herself to be guided to their destination. She sagged a little when she noticed their trajectory was taking them to a shabby collection of Shade-side high-rise micro-apartments.

"I've been worse places." She said, but Ade couldn't believe it. She was too pretty, too pristine a girl to have been anywhere worse than the building he called home.

"Have you really?" He asked.

"No." She said flatly, checking her watch, "You've an hour left with me. Shall we go up?"

The lift creaked and the light inside had gone out. They stood in dark silence as it rumbled upward. On the fifteenth floor it stopped with a jarring thud, and as the doors scraped open, Petunia was through them in a heartbeat, "You ride in that deathtrap every day?"

Ade shrugged, "Taking the stairs is more of a risk." Without elaborating further, he crossed the hall and unlocked his door.

One room. He lived in a cramped and untidy single room, where the furniture and appliances folded out of cupboards in the walls, floor, and ceiling. The bed, Ade pulled from the wall, and it hinged down, filling most of the room. Petunia was forced to stand on a thin strip of floor by the dark, frost covered window, while Ade fussed about. The Scandinavian chill of his Shade-side micro-apartment made her shiver, and she rubbed her arms to keep warm, her silk blouse providing precious little insulation.

Tired of waiting for Ade to finish fussing about neatening up the place, Petunia pulled down her skirt, revealing that she had foregone underwear. Ade's mouth fell open. She pushed him onto the hard mattress, and straddled him.

He gulped nervously, blushing, "You're so different to the other girls." He said, as she undid his tie.

"I'll say." She smirked.

Ade tried to undo his belt, but Petunia batted away his hands, "Let me do my job." She scolded him.

Nodding, he lay his hands down on the mattress. Petunia's orange fingernails worked quickly, undoing all the buttons and zips that held Ade into his clothes. His body resembled an uncooked sausage under his stiff suit; pink, blotchy, and formless. She had hoped he'd at least have a little appealing muscle definition.

He gasped as she yanked down his y-fronts, and he excitedly reached up to cup her breasts. Again, she batted away his hands, shifting her weight to better position herself on top of him.

"I'm really not like the other girls." She said, as she moved forward and enveloped him in a way he had never experienced before, "not like the other girls at all."

She opened her mouth wide, wide, wider, wider! It was full of row upon row of needle-sharp teeth. As Ade, eyes closed, rapidly climaxed, she bit off his head. His neck spurted crimson streams across the wall, as his limbs twitched in ecstasy and death. After a few moments, his headless body went limp, and Petunia dismounted. She dressed, still chewing, crunching up his head into small mushy chunks. When she finally swallowed him down, she checked her reflection in the dark window, wiping some blood from her lips, before slipping away.

"Sex and dinner." He had said.

"In that order?" She had asked.

*

Mr Ripe would ponder aloud most of the next day on why Adrian Cribbage was not at work, all while tutting over the newspaper.

"Have you seen this?" He would ask any of his employees that happened by his open office door, "Damn Mantid attacks, right here on Mercury! The audacity! As if we don't suffer enough, living on this damned rock." He tutted and sighed, "Where *has* Adrian Cribbage got to?" He paused, staring at the article before him, and a terrible thought occurred, "Would someone please call in on him at home and check he's ok? Right away."

Crazy Mal's Used Car Lot

"Who were those beatniks?" Mal's secretary asked, as he returned to the office. It was a static caravan at the edge of the lot, and it was always too hot.

"Didn't like to ask." He said, scratching his balding head, "Seemed in a bit of a hurry." In his other hand he carried a leather satchel, which he laid on her desk.

"Was the hairy one a Glome? Don't see many of them around." The secretary remarked.

Mal nodded, "Did a part exchange on their old banger for a sleek speedster. Paid the difference in cash." He opened the satchel, and spun it around to show her the stacks of bound paper bills. Her eyes widened in surprise, "Who has that much hard cash ready to hand over like that?" She asked, rising in surprise.

"People who don't like too many questions asked, methinks." Mal closed the satchel and locked it away in the safe fitted into the floor.

"You'd better sell that vehicle of theirs sharpish then." She said, moving to peer out of the window at the rusty object in question, "In case it's hot."

Mal nodded, "I'll give it a once over, a lick of paint and a quick service, and it'll be out of here before we know it. It's retro, but not vintage yet, so it might be hard to shift without doing it up." He scratched at the few hairs that lay across his shiny dome, "You take off early. I'll get a head start on getting it done."

Appreciating the early finish, the secretary scooped up her belongings, and bid her boss a good night.

Mal changed out of his grey suit and into his grey overalls. They were stained by oil and grease and had patched knees. He heaved his tool belt into place, and set the coffee machine burbling. He'd need a coffee to keep him going into the evening. It had been a slow day, and he wasn't a young man any more.

He flicked a switch before he left the office, and the illuminated sign at the entrance to his lot went out. It was stained by dust and age, and in need of repair. But times were tough, and it could wait. 'Crazy Mal's Used Car Lot' used to be THE place to buy your nearly-new motors. But the asteroid colonies weren't doing so well since Mercury's banking collapse, and all those settlement loans vanished. He gazed out at the night sky, a glittering view of stars and dust. Chunks of rock bigger than moons, and craggier than mountains drifted by. The sun was too far away to afford them any true day or night. So they made their own. The solar lamps were dimming, letting Mal know it was 6pm, when he finally made his way to the banger that had so recently been left behind by the hasty trio. A Glome; all white fur and teeth. A Trixoloti, its jellyfish head a mesmerising display of natural light. And a Vorpian; a tiny bearded brute who wouldn't look out of place stood motionless in someone's front garden. Never a more peculiar trio had Mal ever seen.

He walked around their vehicle and gave it a good eyeballing. A Fling Standard model, with minor upgrades. He opened the door and peered inside. There was a concerted effort to model these short-range motors after old Earth cars. This one was built to resemble a 1980s Volkwagen Golf, with only a handful of extra switches and dials added to control travel in the vacuum of space. It looked every bit like a run of the mill automobile.

Mal had many from this era in his lot at present. The fashion for them was fading, and being replaced by the bubble-domes and sleek chrome lines of the next generation's taste for high velocity travel. He worried that they would fall out of fashion completely, leaving him cursed with a lot of unsellable junk.

Thud.

His thoughts interrupted, he put down his coffee cup on the boot of the Fling Standard, "Hello? Anyone there?" He peered into the growing gloom.

There was no one else around. Across from the lot the noises from the local drinking hole were starting up, and the constant rumble of passing asteroids vibrated the ground with a gentle familiarity.

Thud.

His coffee mug shook.

Approaching it cautiously, he bent forward and watched it.

Thud.

Again, the cup shook, and wobbled. He grabbed it, and lifted it up, peering into it.

Thud.

"Mmmm-nmmm fmmmmf!" Came a voice from the boot.

Mal fumbled the keys from his pocket, unlocked it and hefted it open. From inside sprung a young woman in an enormous dress. It was lacy and glittery, and covered in muck. Her hands were tied and her mouth was gagged. He pulled the wad of fabric from her mouth, and she spat on the floor, "About time! Do you know how long I've been stuck in there?"

Flapping his jaw up and down, Mal struggled for words. He'd found many surprising things left behind in part-exchange cars before. But never a living person!

"Are you going to untie me or stare at me agog forever?" She waved her bound hands in Mal's face.

In a bubble-domed, sleek, chromed speedster, there was an argument occurring.

"What do you mean you didn't pack the princess?" The little Vorpian jumped up and down in a rage, snatching off his pointy hat and crushing it beneath his boots.

"It wasn't my job!" The Trixoloti glubbed, its luminous head flashing red in frustration.

"Grrr." Growled the hairy Glome.

"Turn this thing around, we have to go back!" The Vorpian began punching whatever was in reach, which happened to be the Glome's thigh.

"Grrrr!" Said the Glome, batting at the tiny fists with its own mighty paws, and sending his much smaller comrade spinning into the footwell.

"How did you leave the princess in the boot? I'm cursed to work with idiots!" The Vorpian screamed, upside down between the Glome's paws.

In the blackness of deep space the sleek bubble-domed vehicle did a three point turn and whizzed back the way it had come.

Mal sat the enormous dress in a plastic chair in his office. Amongst it somewhere the young woman was berating him.

"You seem to be under the impression that I'm in cahoots with the kidnappers?" He said, in a brief pause.

"Well aren't you? You look the sort." She scowled at him over mounds of velvet and taffeta.

"No."

"Oh."

"Three guys came to do a part exchange. Packed up hastily into their new car and took off. They must have forgotten you." He shrugged, offering her a mug of coffee, which she eyed suspiciously.

"Forgot me? Forgot me!" She stamped her feet and her cheeks went a furious red, "I am Princess Agonia! It's insult enough to have been kidnapped, but to then have been abandoned - oh that is simply too much!"

He retracted his arm which held the mug of coffee. If she didn't want it, he would happily drink it. Before he could bring it to his lips, she snatched it from him and downed a mouthful. At once, she spat it all over the floor, "Poison!" She screamed.

"It's not that bad." Mal said defensively, eyeing the steaming brown stain on the carpet.

"I can't stay here. You must take me home at once." Agonia folded her arms and glared at Mal, "I demand your best carriage!"

"Carriage?" Mal was confused, "I've not got anything fancy." He looked out of the window, and wondered if she'd be happy with any of the budget motors he had in stock. Likely not.

"Your finest carriage, and your swiftest driver. I demand simply the best."

Mal was beginning to understand the reason for the gag.

"Where's home?" He asked.

"As if you don't know!" She snorted, "I am princess of the asteroid belt! Take me to my palace! Mother and Father must be worried sick!"

"I've lived in the belt my whole life." Mal said, sitting down, "And I've never heard of us having a royal family. It's a bit like the wild west out here."

"What's a wild west?"

"It's um… never mind." Mal thought it easier if he changed the subject, "I'm not sure where your palace is, so if you're able to find it on a map, that'd be helpful." Reaching into a cabinet, he located an old paper map. He unfolded it across his desk, and waved his hands as he spoke, "This is the belt." The map was a ring of smaller maps. Each one indicating a different settlement on the more sizeable asteroids, "It's a bit old, so might be a smidge out of date. But a palace can't have sprung up overnight. I'm sure you'll be able to find it here somewhere."

Agonia looked from the map to Mal, and back again, "I don't know." She said, "I've never been outside the palace garden! You should know where your monarch lives! It baffles me how you can be so ignorant of a fact that every citizen should know."

Mal pointed to the map, "We are here, in Delton, that's the next settlement over, Bouyville. Have a look at the place names around the map. Something might look familiar." He crossed to the window and sipped his own coffee, gazing out at the night sky. A splinter of silver was swinging between the boulders and rocks overhead. The speedster he sold in exchange for the Fling Standard!

"I think your friends are coming back to get you." He said.

"My friends?" Agonia snorted, "Who even knows I'm here?"

"I meant 'friends' sarcastically."

Agonia rolled her eyes, "Daddy says that sarcasm is the lowest form of wit."

"I'm sure he does. But unless you want to be re-kidnapped, you need to hide. Now."

"I'm not getting into a car boot again! And don't think of squishing me into a cupboard. My dress is mucky enough as it is."

Mal eyed the enormous gown, "It's also very conspicuous."

"It's a genuine Oola Paloola. A one of a kind."

"Very nice. Take it off."

Agonia stood up rigid, "Excuse me!"

"Unless you want them to find you and snatch you off again, take it off. My secretary keeps some spare clothes here, in that closet. Change into something else, quickly."

"I usually have maids who dress and undress me."

Mal peeked out of the window. The kidnappers would be landing any moment, "Just do it!" He shouted, startling the young woman into action. He flung a pale blue skirt and jacket at her, as well as an assortment of other items he assumed a young woman would need. As soon as she was free of the dress, Mal began forcing it into the waste compactor. The device was usually used for household rubbish, and ground noisily as the expensive dress was fed into it.

"My Oola Paloola!" Agonia screamed, trying to snatch it back.

"Do you want to be kidnapped?" Mal snapped. His need to help this brat was a surprise to him. He put it down to his inherent good nature, and not at all the prospect of a reward for returning a Princess to her family, having rescued her from vicious and villainous kidnappers!

Almost changed, Mal picked Agonia up and began shoving her out of a rear window.

"What are you doing?" She demanded.

"I'll hold them up. You go across the way to that bar. You see it?"

Agonia nodded, "Is it... safe?"

"Act casual, and get going! I'll meet you there in a few minutes." Mal shut the window.

Agonia, unevenly buttoned into a skirt and suit jacket, and wearing odd shoes, made her way towards the bar. It was strung about with multicoloured bulbs on strings, and the parking lot was empty save for a handful of hovering motorcycles. The sound of music and laughter emanated warmly from the thin metal walls.

A burbling hum, followed by a crunch behind her made her start, and she looked over her shoulder. The kidnappers had landed, and were falling over each other to climb out of the speedster. Remembering to act casual, she turned back to the bar and strode on. There was a swiftness to her steps, which turned into a flailing dash when she reached the parking lot. She crossed the tarmac in a few seconds and threw herself through the door.

The Glome moved slowly and deliberately, "Grrr-rrr." He said, indicating the open, empty boot of the Fling Standard.

The Vorpian screamed like a boiling kettle, his fists bunched, while the Trixoloti drifted about, his head radiating a perplexed purple.

"I'm afraid I don't give refunds." Mal said as he emerged from the office, "Sold as seen. What can I do for you?"

"Grr-rrrrr." The Glome grumbled.

"You left something behind?" Mal echoed.

"Grrrrrr!"

"Something valuable? Oh dear! Maybe I can help you find it. Did you drop it under a seat maybe?" Mal deliberately walked past the open boot, paying it no attention at all.

The black varnished door swung stiffly open, and Agonia leapt inside. She steadied her pace, and strode within, paused, and put her hands on her hips, looking haughtily about the bar. Gathering herself, she steadied her breathing. The bar was dark, smelled vaguely of vomit and disinfectant, and the carpet beneath her feet was sticky. No one looked at her.

Struggling to correctly re-button her jacket, she moved to the bar and plonked herself on one of the worn stools that just about stood there.

"What'll it be?" Asked the woman behind the bar. She wore leopard print, and had her hair done up in a tall blonde spiral, her face caked in rosey makeup.

"Champagne." Agonia said.

The woman laughed at her, something Agonia had never experienced before. She found it quite the affront.

"You'll be lucky!" The woman jangled with all the costume jewellery she wore.

"Whatever you have that is worthy of a princess."

The woman in leopard print smiled, "Cinzano and lemonade?"

"Why not?"

The minute Vorpian, held at head-height by the Glome, jabbed a finger in Mal's face, "Where is she?"

"She?" Mal had backed up to the wall of the lot, and was now pinned there by the criminal trio.

"You know who!" The Vorpian ground his teeth so loud it made Mal wince.

"Look, I don't know what you're talking about!" Mal lied quite convincingly, "There was nothing and no one in the car when I came out to start work on it. The boot was open and the doors unlocked. That's all I know."

The Trixoloti glittered as he drifted back and forth, thinking.

Mal was good at telling lies - he had to be, in the used car business, "There's a regular bus that comes through each evening about the time you left, runs up through the next few asteroids and back. Only a few small settlements. If you hurry, you might catch up to it. If there was someone in the car, they won't have got far.

The Vorpian grabbed Mal's face in his tiny round hands, "If I find out you're lying, we'll be back in a flash, and I'll stamp on your head until you're dead. It'll be a long, slow, painful, crunchy kind of death. Understand?"

Mal nodded, his cheeks squashed by tiny fists.

"Grrr-rrr-grrrrrr." The Glome said menacingly as he placed the Vorpian on the floor.

The three of them climbed back into their sleek speedster, and once they had whooshed away, Mal allowed himself to breathe. Then he dashed out of the lot to the bar.

Behind the bar, the woman with the spiral hair was eyeing Agonia warily.

"Evening, Dreardre. Hope she's been behaving herself." Mal said as he hurried across the sticky carpet.

"She's your latest secretary?" Dreadre scowled at Mal.

"No no..." He said, turning quickly away, and attempting to scoop the princess from the bar. But the young woman was limp, and giggling.

"How much have you had?" He asked the intoxicated girl.

"She's not even finished her first." Dreadre said.

Mal watched Agonia's eyes sway independently as she tried to focus on him, "Take me somewhere cosy." She slurred.

Propping her up under one arm, he escorted Agonia from the bar.

Half way across the road she gave up walking and sat down. Plonking herself on the asphalt, she refused to budge, and became a dead weight.

"They're not even bothered." She muttered.

"Come on, let's not sit here. We'll get run over. Up you get!"

Agonia slapped away his hands as he tried to grip her, "Peasant, gerroff! Don't you touch my royal personage!"

"How did you get so drunk on a couple of sips?" Mal gave up trying to lift the princess onto her feet, instead pacing back and forth. What was to be done?

Agonia lay back on the road, starfished on the cracked black surface, "Have you ever been kidnapped?"

"Can't say I have." Mal rubbed his head.

"I have."

"I know."

"Not this time. Not today. Before."

"This isn't the first time you've been kidnapped?"

Agonia giggled, "I've lost count. Fifty ninety three and a half times. Today is the half." Mal bent over and began to roll the princess across the road towards his lot, "Wheeeeeee!" She said, as she rolled limply over and over at Mal's urgent shoving.

When she bumped into the curb on the far side, she pushed him away, and made a show of righting herself, eventually sitting on the pavement, her feet in the gutter.

"I'd have thought there would be better security around a princess." Mal sat next to her.

"I'm fed up with it. I've never seen anything of the universe! Do you want to know a secret? Shh, you mustn't tell a soul!"

"I'm all ears."

"I let myself be kidnapped. I stand near open windows, and leave castle doors unlocked, and linger by the tall trees at the edge of the walled castle garden."

"Why?"

"Boredom, mainly. Being a princess is so dull!"

"You must have had a few adventures then, if you keep letting yourself be kidnapped and ransomed back again?"

"Pfft, hardly!" Agonia dribbled slightly as she scoffed, "I only ever see the inside of a car boot, or a van, or a warehouse. Then when my ransom is paid, I'm bundled back into the castle again to be ignored by my parents until the next kidnap."

"You want them to pay you some attention? Is that it?"

"But they don't. They act all grateful and weepy when I'm returned to them. But it's all for show. The minute we've finished waving to the spectators and come in off the balcony I'm sent to my room, and they vanish off to theirs, and they avoid me at all costs."

"Doesn't sound like much fun being a princess."

"I don't want to be a princess."

"What do you want to be?"

Agonia was sobering up a little, and she gazed with new focus into the rocky heavens above, "I want to be an explorer, like in the early days of colonising the solar system. I want to see things. I want to have experiences! I want to live a life worth living."

Mal found himself sympathetic to the frustrated girl, sighing, and heaving himself up onto his feet, "Come along, let's get you something to eat, and we can sort out some kind of a plan to get you home."

"Home!" Agonia spat, "Didn't you hear anything I just said?"

Mal didn't know what else to do. The dastardly trio wouldn't be gone for long, and she needed to be away before they returned.

"I heard you perfectly." Said a voice from across the road.

With the click-click-click of high heeled shoes, Dreadre stalked across the road. Her horn-rimmed glasses shone like cat's eyes in the evening gloom.

"Who are you?" Agonia asked, dragging herself upright, using Mal as a climbing frame.

"We've met already, though not formally. Dreadre Nose, landlady, entrepreneur..."

"And secretive schemer of nefarious schemes." Mal finished for her.

Dreadre mock-curtseyed, her oily lipstick glowing, "I couldn't help but overhear what you were saying."

"That'll happen when eavesdropping." Agonia said.

"Quite right. Now, forgive me for being so bold, but I have a business proposition for you. Both of you. Come back to the bar and hear me out."

"Don't trust her." Mal said, "She'll serve you beer just as soon as poison you, depending on which will benefit her best."

Dreadre was flattered, "You old charmer. Come along."

Click-click-click her heels carried her away.

*

The bus driver whimpered, gripped in the Glome's clawed paws.

"He doesn't know anything." The Trixoloti said, drifting away.

Furrowing his bushy eyebrows, the Vorpian ground his teeth together, "We've been lied to! That guy from the car dealership."

"Grr." The Glome dropped the sobbing, bruised bus driver, and returned to the sleek speedster.

Across from the bus-stop stood a row of shops, and one of them had caught the Vorpian's attention. The shop fronts were illuminated by the feeble street lamps, and in the barred window display of one the Vorpian spied a series of firearms racked up beside ammunition and photos of hunters and their trophies.

"It's high time I invested in some decent weaponry." He stood on his tiptoes to peer in the window, "That one." He said, pointing at an enormous plasma rifle.

The Trixoloti unfurled a series of jelly fronds through the letterbox, creeping them around and into the window display. Grabbing a selection of guns, he then tried and failed to slide them out through the letterbox.

"Um…" He said, "This isn't going to work."

One of the Glome's fists broke the glass of the window, and bent the bars. He snatched up two big armfulls of the weapons as the shop alarm began to blare.

*

Dreadre had taken them into a back room of the bar, where the carpet wasn't quite so sticky, and the air wasn't quite so smelly. It looked like a store room, refitted with a table and chairs into a back-room poker den.

"Let me see if I understand you correctly," Agonia summarised, "You want to ransom me back to my parents. But not really? You want to split the money, and then let me go?"

Dreadre nodded, "It's a serious offer. I get a payout for keeping quiet about your location, and Mal's involvement, and you get funds to start up a life you want away from the life of a princess. Everyone wins."

"It seems too good to be true." Mal was deeply suspicious of Dreadre.

"It's either that, or I report your whereabouts to the authorities."

"What would you get out of that?" Mal asked, "You don't do anything without it benefitting you."

"There's a reward for information leading to the safe return of the princess. But it's nowhere near as much as I could make demanding a ransom, even if it is split two ways."

"Three." Mal said.

"Two." Dreadre corrected, "Half for me, half for you two. That's the deal. Take it or leave it."

Their meeting was interrupted by a knock at the door.

"Yes?" Dreadre shouted.

"Sorry boss," Said a meek staff member as he opened the door, "But we've a spot of bother."

Through the crack of the open door, Mal recognised who was causing the bother.

"Your friends are back." He said to Agonia.

The princess turned to Dreadre, "If you help me shake those three, we have a deal." And she held out a hand to shake.

Ignoring the hand, and smiling with one side of her mouth, Dreadre rose and left the room.

"I really wouldn't trust her if I were you." Mal said, nervously biting his fingernails.

"Why? What do you have against her?" Agonia whispered, moving to the closed door and pressing an ear against it.

"She's my ex-wife." Mal said.

Dreadre flashed her brightest and most dangerous smile at the Vorpian, the Glome, and the Trixoloti. They loitered in the doorway, glowering. Around the room, the leather and denim clad patrons tensed their fists and flexed their biceps. Several members of the local biker gang considered Dreadre's their local, and wouldn't have her messed with. She served them cheap beer and overlooked the majority of their indiscretions, after all.

"Can I help you?" She asked, her voice sugary.

The Vorpian said, "I hope so." And strode forward. He marched up to Dreadre, which took quite a while on his inch-long legs, and glared up at her.

In reply, she peered over her bosom at him, "How much does it take to get a Vorpian pissed? I've not got any thimbles to serve you with."

This got a rumble of laughter from the shaggy and tattooed man around the room. Men who, in the darkness, were alert and closing their fists around anything they might use as a weapon. It wasn't the

Vorpian that worried them, but the huge brutish Glome stood stoically blocking the door.

"We're looking for someone. A girl. She's… important to us." The Vorpian said.

"You're looking in the wrong boozer." Dreadre said, "It's mostly geezers, blokes, lads, and dads I get in here. Not a delicate scene, this one."

The Vorpian quickly counted the tense bodies around the room, and figured it wouldn't be a fair fight, "You look like you might be a shrewd businesswoman."

"I might be." She said, folding her arms.

"In which case, perhaps I can cut a deal with you. She's worth quite a lot of money, that girl. A portion of which could be yours." The Vorpian was holding his impatience down well. He wanted to kick and scream and bite her feet off and stamp on her eyes. But he bit his tongue, and played the criminal game of 'who can out-think the other'.

"That is an interesting offer, and I might take you up on it…" Dreadre said, "If it wasn't for the fact that I have no idea who you're talking about. Now, I'll ask you once, and once only to either buy a drink and play nice with the locals, or to get out of my pub."

The Vorpian's face bloomed red with barely concealed rage, but he managed to say, "We'll have three pints of whatever you've on draught that passes as lager."

Dreadre nodded, and moved behind the bar. It wasn't until the pints had been pulled, and the three interlopers had placed themselves at a corner table, that the others around the room allowed themselves to relax. And even then, they kept their improvised weapons to hand.

"Turn up the juke box!" She called across the room, "Let's have something that rocks."

The nearest biker to the machine slid in a coin, and jabbed a couple of buttons. An EP slid and slapped from a rotating selection, and a needle dropped into place. The room was filled with the clashing rock and roll of *Nancy And The Pants*.

"I love this song." Dreadre said, humming along to the classic rock and roll anthem.

The sound of the music masked the sound of the back door slamming shut.

Mal and Agonia ran around the building, keeping low as they passed the windows. Mal bobbed up long enough to see where the trio of ne'er-do-wells were seated.

"Keep low, this way."

"Why are we running away?" Agonia hissed, "Dreadre is going to get rid of them isn't she?"

"It's the uncertainty around how exactly she'll get rid of them that worries me." In his lot he could see the sleek silver, bubble-domed speedster the trio had bought from him. An idea formed in his mind, and he urgently hurried Agonia on.

Nursing their pints, the Glome and the Trixoloti said very little. The Vorpian gulped his pint through a straw, muttering darkly under his breath. Beside their table, a dirty window looked out over a row of parked motorbikes and to Mal's unlit lot.

"Say, look at that." The Trixoloti said, glowing curiously yellow, "Someone's trying to get into our car!"

The Vorpian spluttered, and jumped onto the window ledge. He pressed his nose against the glass, misting it with his hot breaths, "It's them! The princess and the car salesman!" He hissed.

Dreadre arrived at their table with another round of pints, "On the house." She said.

The Glome reared, batting away the tray, sending amber liquid and glass in all directions, "Grrr!" He growled, reaching into his thick white coat and pulling out a tiny pistol. It was far too small for his massive paw, yet he held it at Dreadre's face.

The Vorpian too had produced a gun. The huge plasma rifle.

"Now where were you hiding that?" Dreadre asked, smirking.

Chairs scraped, glasses were placed loudly on tables, and pool cues were slapped meaningfully against palms, as the bikers and assorted others in the bar made their presence felt. They moved forward slowly, crowding in around the terrible trio.

"Put them away, boys." She said, holding her hands out, "You don't want things to get messy, do you?"

The Vorpian grinned viciously, and fired his gun.

The boom shook the cars in the lot, and Agonia screamed in fright. Mal looked up in time to see the corner of Dreadre's bar blow outward, as the Vorpian flew through it, propelled by the push-back from the plasma rifle. In the illuminated hole stood Dreadre, aiming her own bosom-holstered piece at the Glome's genitals, and holding the Trixoloti by the fronds.

Finally getting the car door open, Mal began rummaging around inside.

"What are you looking for?" She asked, "Shouldn't we get back there and help, or something?"

Mal shook his head, "Dreadre's fine. Trust me. A-ha!" Locating whatever it was he was hunting for, he yanked something large and heavy from below the back seat, and waddled as fast as he could to his office. Agonia waited by the speedster, watching as the bar fight spilled out into the road. The Vorpian was buried beneath brick and rubble, the Trixoloti had been deflated, yet the Glome roared and fought on still with its teeth and claws. The bikers had quickly disarmed the Glome in the moment of shock that followed the rifle blast. The Juke Box had had it, taking the brunt of the plasma stream. The EP currently playing wound slowly to a distorted finish.

Mal returned to Agonia's side to watch the fight slowly wind up. The Glome and the Trixoloti were bound and shoved into a corner of the bar, a corner that Mal knew had particularly sticky carpets. The Glome's fur would never be the same again.

"Ok, let's head back."

"Back?" But we've just run away from there?" Agonia was very confused.

"Don't worry about it." Mal said, and made his way back towards Dreadre's.

The rubble shifted, and the Vorpian emerged, gasping. He went unnoticed, as had the Glome's discarded weapon. The small laser pistol. The Vorpian crawled towards it, trying not to make a sound. He picked it up, and aimed it with shaking hands at Dreadre's back.

But he didn't get chance to fire it, as Agonia kicked him clear across the room. She screamed as she did so, putting all of her frustration and fear into it. The Vorpian sailed across the room, bouncing a couple of times before skidding to a halt on the dance floor.

Dreadre smiled an impressed little smile.

*

The sun-lamps slowly came to life, giving the asteroid colonies a morning.

"I've had word," Dreadre said, "The ransom isn't being paid."

Agonia was aghast, "They're not paying my ransom?"

They were sat in Mal's office, as Dreadre's bar had been closed for renovation work.

Mal read the message that had been received, "They've been deposed."

"How?"

"Violently." Dreadre said, "So it seems you're not a princess any more."

Mal put the message down, "Sounds like they were making the citizens pay your ransom each time. They finally got tired of it, and revolted."

"But I've been gone less than a day!" Agonia was limp in her chair.

Crouching down to the safe in the floor, Mal said, "All is not lost."

"There's no point looking in there. You never kept anything in it except old receipts." Dreadre sniffed, but her eyes went wide when he pulled out the enormous carry-all he had pilfered from the trio's speedster.

"I don't really know how they came by it, but I'm quite glad I had the foresight to liberate it when I did." He unzipped the bag and stacks of notes fell out, cascading across the floor.

Dreadre reached forward, but Mal held her wrist, stopping her getting too close, "How much would your share of the random have been?"

Dreadre told him, and Mal counted out double that from the carry-all and handed it to her. She eyed the rest of the money greedily, "What about the rest?" She asked.

Mal counted out a similar amount again twice, once for himself, and the second time for Agonia.

Agonia held the money oddly, never having needed to use it for herself before, "How much is this?"

"Plenty to get yourself set up somewhere nice. Or a decent little ship to go off exploring in." Mal grinned, "Go and have a life!"

53

The Red Wind

"Your bodies are now the property of the Martian Penal Corporation. Free will is no longer yours to exercise. Autonomy is forbidden. You will obey, until the end of your life, whether that be through causes natural or otherwise. Proceed."

The loudspeaker gave the same grim greeting to every new cattle-wagon of chained and unwashed detainees; Wide, scared eyes, torn and soiled clothes, adults and children alike. There was no mercy from the Earth Judicial Authority, no explanation, no appeals, no warning of the black-clad visitors in the night.

Manacled feet shuffled forward, inch by inch through the back-and-forth aisle made of corrugated metal sheeting and barbed wire. No one had the energy to speak. And what was there left to say? All talking had done was to further terrify everyone on the month-long voyage. They had been packed in with little room to move, nowhere approaching a sanitary latrine, no food, little water, and one tiny window. It was through that small oblong patch of thick glass that they first caught sight of the approaching red dot. The planet Mars. That was when it all became clear. Shrieks and cries filled the close and humid space, as the realisation sunk in.

By the end of the voyage, the number of living persons aboard had dropped by a fifth.

Person by person the line moved forward. At the head of the line, a cluster of heavily armed guards dressed down each beleaguered and malnourished individual. All handled with the same rough disregard.

"Name?"

"Gabriel."

"Full name."

"Gabriel Hernandes."

Buttons were punched, a computer whirred and ticked as it processed data and spat out a coloured plastic band. The band was strapped tightly to the prisoner's left wrist, and their chains removed.

"You are now Inmate 71313-13. Unlucky." The processing guard laughed without humour.

The band on Gabriel's arm pinched tightly, and was a bright sky blue.

"Political prisoners are housed in Blue Zone, on the fourth level. Go." The guards wagged their guns in the direction Gabriel should proceed. Before moving, he paused to look at the band, and wonder what it was that classed him as a political prisoner.

The impatient pressure of a muzzle in the small of his back made him hurry on his way, glad to be free of the heavy chains, but fearful of what lay ahead.

"Name?"

"Tove Lisesdotter."

Again the computer clacked and ticked and whirred, before spitting out a pink band.

"You are now inmate 71313-14."

"I am not." Tove replied, head held high, defiant but shaking, "I demand to know why I am here."

The butt of a gun answered her question, cracking her nose and loosening several teeth. She cried out as she fell into the line of people chained at her back. They caught her as best they could. She slumped to the floor, stunned, holding her face as crimson blood began to spill from her nostrils.

"How dare you!" She tried to shout, but her voice came out a strangled whine.

The guards dragged her forward, unchained her, and strapped the pink band tightly to her wrist before shoving her onward, "Gender and Sexual non-conformists in Pink Zone. Seventh level. Get out of my sight."

Tove appealed to those awaiting processing, but they shrank back, looking at the floor, unwilling to face the guards, "There is more of us than them!" Her voice cracked, "They can't do this. It's inhuman."

The guard who appeared to be in charge of the processing fired a single shot, exploding Tove's left knee. She screamed, collapsing to the floor, as more of her vital blood erupted from her.

"Next." The guard said, ignoring Tove's wailing.

Next in line was a child, no more than ten years old.

"Name?"

Tove's screams echoed through the hot metal corridors of the Martian prison city.

*

There were whispers. There were always whispers. No one knew exactly what, or who, or where it was. Was it a way out? A secret community of escaped prisoners? A chance for a new life? No one seemed to know. Every few months graffiti would appear on walls or cell doors; A red circle with three wavy lines across it. It was known as the Red Wind. And when the Red Wind appeared, something happened. Sometimes inmates would vanish. Other times extra rations of food, inveigled from the guard's lavish kitchens, would appear in cells. Or medicine would be miraculously dispensed to those in need. Other times it would be outlawed music played through the loud speakers, or recorded messages of hope. The prison guards were at a loss as to how to stop these odd occurrences. Punishments would double in the days following the appearance of the Red Wind. Patrols would be tripled. And then eventually return to normal, only for another incident to enrage them once more.

"It's been like this for years. Decades even." Tove said, nursing her aching knee. It had healed crooked, and she now walked with a limp, "It was going on well before I arrived."

She sat at a table in the noisy and over-packed canteen amidst a huddle of other hungry and desperate inmates. Most of them new arrivals, rubbing their wrists where the pink band cut into their flesh.

"Five minutes, perverts." Shouted a patrolling guard from his elevated walkway. His gun scanned them lazily, with a finger resting on the trigger, "Then back to your cells."

Lunch was a hurried meal, with scarcely any time for chat.

"When the Red Wind blows, keep your heads down, be good, do what the guards tell you, and you won't be the ones to suffer."

"Why don't they stop, if everything they do only makes it worse for everyone?" Asked a terrified young man with a black eye.

"Or why don't they really fuck around with the guards? If they can do all you say they must have access to all kinds of areas of the city, and systems. They could set us all free!" A young woman said, jabbing her finger against the table top.

Tove smiled slightly, this was someone whose spirit would not be broken easily. She was feisty, and Tove liked her, "I suspect," She shrugged at the young man, "It's for a greater good."

The young man snorted, "This is a death sentence; being here. A drawn out, dirty, shameful way to go."

"Why were you sent here?" Tove asked.

"Got accused of staring at the other guys in the locker room at the gym."

"And were you?"

"No!"

The lie was blatant.

"I started a lesbian zine; *Dyke Daily*." The young woman said proudly, "Copied and printed it in my cellar. Spreading literature of 'radical acceptance' got me bagged and gagged in the middle of the night."

"Time's up." The guard shouted, and reluctantly the inmates began to clear from the room.

Trove patted the young woman on the shoulder, "What's your name?"

"Fox."

"Good to meet you Fox. Keep that fighting spirit." And to the young man she said, "Never be ashamed of who you are. There was once a time where people like us were accepted, celebrated even."

"Ancient history." He snorted.

"And what's your name?"

"Garth."

"It's not so bleak as you think, Garth. I have faith that the Red Wind, whoever they are, will win out, and set us all free one day." Tove turned and limped stiffly to her cell. Garth rolled his eyes.

*

A few days later, as the morning klaxon sounded, and the cell doors in the Pink Zone trembled open, gasps and muttered curses filled Tove's ears like shifting sand. Pushing off her thin bed frame, Tove peered out onto the landing. The cells were arranged in stacked rings, with walkways and rusty stairs circling a central open space.

"Paska!" Tove swore in surprise.

A huge banner had been hung in the central void of the Pink Zone overnight. It was black, and hand painted across it in bold red lines was the sign of the Red Wind.

"What does it mean?" Fox asked, sidling up.

Tove bit her lip, scanning the walkways across from her cell; those above, those below, "All the men are gone." She said, wrinkling her forehead.

"But... how?" Fox leaned over the railing, glaring in all directions. It was true. Half of the cells were empty, and those that remained were all women, or variations thereof.

Within minutes the guards came stamping through Pink Zone, shoving the inmates back into their cells and locking the doors. Shouting and swearing could be heard ricocheting back and forth for the rest of the day, and the cells were not opened again for lunch, or for dinner, or for the women to use the exercise yard.

All day long Tove listened at her cell door, catching snippets of conversation. The guards were clueless. The men had simply vanished into thin air.

*

Garth woke up and blinked his eyes. The light made him squint, and the dry air had parched his tongue. He sat up and gazed about. He was laid over some kind of rock formation, and he was outside. The sky was a pale yellow, and the rocks and dust were shades of brown and red. He wasn't the only one currently stirring, and finding themselves in this strange new place. Men were strewn all about him, as if they were still in their bunks.

"Where am I?" Garth mumbled, as he tried to form spit to moisten his dry tongue and lips.

Someone came running around the edge of the formation, panting, sweating, stumbling. He tripped over someone's feet, and landed heavily in the dirt.

Rushing over, Garth helped him up, "What's happened? Are you ok?" He asked the terrified man.

But the man was wide-eyed and wild, fighting to be free of Garth's grip. He was no sooner stood upright, than he was off again, staggering as fast as he could into the bleak wilderness. Garth could see nothing in pursuit of the man, and so followed his footprints the way he had come.

The other men stirring around him seemed as confused as he was. Some were sat, puzzled and mute. Others had begun to wander about. Some were bunched together, talking urgently in low voices.

Garth ignored them, and allowed his curiosity to lead him on.

As he navigated the boulders and shifting sand, he stumbled upon a cave. But an unusual cave. The entrance was rectangular, and there seemed to be evidence of ancient carvings, eroded by time. The wind changed direction, and from above he heard the familiar sound of the Penal colony klaxon.

High up on a rocky outcrop above the cave sat the engorged bulk of the prison. Garth wandered how he, and all the other men from the Pink Zone had miraculously, and without any apparent effort, escaped.

The cave beckoned to him, and it seemed to have a similar effect on the others, who in dribs and drabs were now following him. Into the darkness they went.

Tove waited for her moment, and grabbed the guard by the wrist, pulling him into her cell.

Once a thorough sweep of the Zone had been completed, the women's cell doors were unlocked again. Tove had watched, and paid attention, and seen something very interesting.

The guard raised his gun, but Tove quickly batted it away, and flattened herself against him, a hand over his mouth, "Tell me about the Red Wind!" She hissed in his face, "There's a small red stain on your wrist that you keep trying to hide. You painted it."

The guard relaxed his gun hand, and raised the other in a supplicating gesture. Cautiously moving from him, she kept a hand on his gun, pointed away. The man nodded, and smiled. It was only now that she was so close to him, that she saw how his skin seemed to gleam greenishly in the yellow light of the overhead bulb. He blinked, and behind his eyelids a second set blinked a moment later.

"We are few. But soon will be many." Said the guard, his tongue flicking oddly as he spoke.

Tove stepped back, "What are you?"

The cave was dark, and descended steeply into an impenetrable blackness. The sound of breathing and footsteps echoed off the smooth walls. Garth found the air to be refreshingly cool and damp, and condensation began to collect on his face. With a terrific clunk, a mechanism engaged and opened a hidden door. Dim orange light crept out, enticing Garth to approach. In the space beyond, which was vast, stood elaborate mechanical devices, with arms weaving back and forth. They stitched together streams of red and pink material that glistened. The air smelled oddly sweet. The door closed behind them.

The guard holstered his gun, as he made to leave Tove's cell, "Our words don't translate exactly, but I am one of the Red Wind. We lived in the air, and in the sea, and in the leaves of this world, until it died. We slept, waiting for a new dawn in which to awaken. We are one, and we are many."

"A Martian?" Tove breathed, "And what are you doing with the prisoners? Are you helping us to escape?"

The guard shrugged, "In a manner of speaking."

Garth gasped as a shifting dune of sand slithered towards him, and rose up into a pillar. It rippled and convulsed, until it had assumed a shape not unlike his own. Many others were rising up from the floor in front of other men. Or drifting from the walls, or falling from the ceiling. The sand-Garth held out an approximation of a hand to real-Garth, who mimicked the gesture.

"Hello." He said, "Who are you?" He had always dreamed of meeting an alien, but never dreamed it would ever happen, and had always imagined little grey men, "I'm Garth."

The shifting sand-person repeated his name back to him in a strange kind of white noise.

"Yeah, Garth. That's me. Who are you?"

Again, the sand said 'Garth'.

In a moment, the pillars of living sand erupted into clouds, and enveloped the humans. They coated them like breadcrumbs, and Garth found himself unable to resist as his dusty coating walked him towards one of the multi-armed machines. The front of the machine opened, and he didn't like the look of the inside. He fought back, tried not to walk, not to move, but the thing that encased him was relentless, and marched him onward. Once inside, the machine closed over him.

"How do you mean?" Tove asked, desperate for answers.

The guard half smiled as he walked away, "You will all soon be freed to begin new lives."

Garth was pulled apart. Cell by cell, and genome by genome, and woven anew. The arms of the machine spooled his tissues into lengths of red and pink fabric, stitching and knotting him back together. But he wasn't the Garth he was before. He was a new Garth. The dust particles of the strange living sand had been woven into him at a genetic level. The Garth that had entered the cave was dead, and this new Garth was someone, and something new. One of the Red Wind.

The next morning, Tove related her conversation with the guard to Fox and an assortment of other trusted individuals, "So we have hope!" She smiled, "And who would have thought that it would be Martians who help to set us free!"

The women began excitedly to talk about home, and the lives they left behind, dreaming of a freedom they would never see.

Stardust And Diamond

"The competition is ramping up, and the stage is set for the last few performances. A truly spectacular location has been selected for the final leg of the 67th Terra-Nova Ice Skating League Tournament. Out of Ninety-nine competing couples, only five are left, and they will all be performing in front of a sell-out crowd of thousands, and a televised crowd that numbers in the billions; upon the rings of Saturn!" The camera panned left from the newscaster, taking in the full scale of the vista at her back. The great mass of Saturn hung like a milky pearl, surrounded by the plateau of glittering, ice encrusted rings.

"How have they managed it?" Asked Diamond, skating to a stop to catch his breath.

"Something to do with gravity satellites?" Shrugged Stardust, tucking a loose curl of hair behind an ear. Her hair was forever escaping the confines of their bobble restraints.

However the enormous rinks were constructed, it wouldn't matter if they didn't perfect the routine. They prepared themselves to go again, moving into position. Stardust set off full tilt for Diamond, who braced for the catch. Stardust hit her mark, leaped, and Diamond caught her in his strong arms. The next move involved a full 360 flip, and, swearing loudly, Diamond's head connected with Stardust's knee. They both collapsed onto the ice, bashing elbows and bums as they fell in a tangled, spangled heap.

"You're distracted." Diamond grumbled as he righted himself, his bladed feet making tiny cuts in the surface of the practice rink, "Sort your head out."

They had been at it all day, and he was at the end of his tether. They both knew that if they continued, there would be a boiling argument that would help neither of them. They had to go and let off steam.

Diamond's skates hissed over the ice as they carried him away, leaving Stardust laid on her back. She balled her fists and hit the ice.

"Tricky move." Said a scratchy little voice.

Stardust sat up, alert. There should be no one else in the practice rink but them. They had it booked all morning.

"Though I thought you'd have nailed it by now." The voice was coming from a tatty little creature, perched on a bench at the side of the rink. His fur was matted, hanging over gleaming yellow eyes. He looked moth-eaten, and scratched at himself intermittently with ivory claws, "That injury must have been more severe than the press let on."

Stardust flinched inwardly at the mention of her recent painful break from intergalactic figure skating. It was the final of last year's League; She had been distracted, something in the crowd reflected light directly into her eyes at a crucial moment, dazzling her, and, well, everyone had seen the clip. It had gone viral.

She glared at the scruffy creature.

"Oh if looks could kill," He chuckled at her, "I'd be down one of my nine lives."

"You're not supposed to be in here. No one is. Private session." She said, standing, and attempting to dismiss the tatty intruder.

"Ratbag."

"Excuse me?"

"That's what they call me."

"Who's 'they'?"

"Whoever they want to be." He winked at her, "And you could be whoever you want to be too, for the right price."

"I don't know what you're trying to sell, but I'm not the buyer you're looking for."

Ratbag shook his head, "I'm never mistaken. Got the nose for it." He twitched his crooked whiskers.

Turning her back on him, Stardust began skating away. Ratbag called to her retreating form, "What if I told you there was a way to nail that move, and have it be no effort at all?"

"I'd say you're delusional." She replied over her shoulder, as her hair broke free from the bobble again.

"It's in pill form. Zero serious side effects, if you're careful."

She spun around to face him, continuing to skate away, backwards, "I'm not a doper. I don't want your drugs."

Ratbag shook a little baggy of green pills in the air, "It's not drugs, Abigail Stardust, it's success."

She shook her head, and something shot across the ice towards her. Ratbag nodded at it; a bag containing a single pill, "Try it. A freebee, to show you my good intentions. Guarantee you'll nail that move first time once you've taken my gift. And if you keep up the dosage, you'll nail it every time."

Ratbag didn't wait for a reply. He hopped down from his perch, and sauntered away, his balding tail twitching. She watched him go, then stared down at the baggy on the ice. She could have turned away and left it behind, but she didn't. Bending down she picked up the pill in its clear plastic pouch, and examined it. A perfect sphere of dusty moss-green powder.

"Success?" She mused, "I doubt it." Clenching the pill in a fist, she left the rink.

Two hours later, Stardust and Diamond reconvened on the ice. He had let off steam by shagging a groupie. Stardust could smell someone else's perfume on him. It didn't smell nice.

"Let's do this." He said, slapping his hands together, "Whoo yeah!"

They skated, and twirled, and leaped, and were graceful as swans. Until the usual point in the routine, where it all went wrong. This time Stardust hit her head on the ice as she fell, and they both swore very loudly.

"Maybe we should simplify the routine." Diamond said, "You clearly can't manage this."

"No." Stardust snapped. "I can do it. I'll get it. I need to win. I need to make this comeback worth it!"

"No one will hold it against you. It's been a tough year. We're already in the top five!"

"Give me a few minutes. Then we'll try again."

"Fine." Diamond snorted, already contemplating replacement moves for the finale of their performance. Nothing would be quite as dramatic as what they already had planned. But he was fine with being in the top 5 this year. Coming first would be nice, but all he really wanted to do was skate and show off and bed all the groupies he could.

In the toilets, Stardust clumped her heavy skates over the thickly matted floor. She ran the water and splashed her face, as her hair fell forward into the sink.

"I can do this." She said it like a mantra, again and again. Then she paused to take the green pill from its hiding place in her cleavage. She stared at it.

'Success' Ratbag had said. She was desperate for the win; To prove those that told her to retire, that they were mistaken. To prove she could still compete and win! She opened the baggy and swallowed the pill, helped down by a handful of water from the tap.

"Success." She said to her reflection.

"Let's do this." She said to Diamond, once back on the ice.

He nodded, and they took up their starting positions. As the performance progressed, Stardust found herself flushed, as her heartbeat quickened. Pins and needles surged over her skin and sweat beaded on her forehead. She began to regret taking the pill, but as soon as the sensation began, it went. In its place was a sure calm. Her legs did what was needed, her arms poised and providing balance with exquisite precision. She moved into the finale with a liquid ease, leaping, twirling, flipping, and landing. Perfection.

"Amazing!" Diamond cheered, bouncing and hugging her tight.

Stardust grinned grimly, "Success." She said.

*

The bar was crowded with competitors, managers, television crews, and other people with official looking tags on lanyards. The day had gone so well, that Stardust and Diamond decided a celebratory drink was in order.

"One more day of practice, before the final leg of the competition!" Someone said.

"It's going to be spectacular!" Said someone else.

Stardust could feel eyes on her, as she sipped her cocktail. It was bright blue and tasted of coconut. Let them stare, let them wonder, let them doubt, she thought. I'm a winner, through and through.

"You ready to invest in your future?" Ratbag said, plonking himself on the seat beside her.

"What are you doing here?" She hissed at him, "Diamond'll be back from the loo any minute. Get away!"

"We've got some time. He's conveniently met someone willing to do very sloppy things to him." Ratbag chuckled, "He'll put it in anything, won't he?"

Stardust sighed. Her skating partner was always getting himself into trouble. A trail of nameless single mothers littered his sequinned path to stardom.

"What do you want?" She asked Ratbag, as he scratched behind his ear.

"What I want is irrelevant. It's what you want. That's what I'm here for."

She was loath to admit that the pill had worked. Whatever it was, it had made her performance effortless, and she could still feel its effects now, albeit lessened. It was like becoming silk.

"What's in that little pill of yours?"

Ratbag tapped his scabby nose, "A secret blend of eleven herbs and spices." He grinned mischievously.

"Seriously."

"A little of this, a little of that. Don't you worry about it. But the effects aren't permanent. Can you feel them fading?"

The feeling the pill had given her was almost gone.

"Maybe a bit." She said, sipping her luminous cocktail.

"Five hundred quid."

"What!" She spat blue across the table.

"You've got one chance at one performance. One chance to get it right. One chance to prove all the nay-sayers wrong." He watched her with those gleaming yellow eyes of his, like he could see into her skull and read her thoughts, "Five hundred quid for success. For your one chance to win this thing, and lift that shiny cup."

"The Ice Chalice is not just a cup."

"Whatever the trinket is, it'll cost you five hundred."

"For how many?"

Ratbag produced a baggy from his pocket. It was stuffed full of tantalising green pills, "For one. But I do have quite a stash, if you're in the market for more. Be careful though. They pack a punch."

She could have told him to do one, to take a hike, to get lost, to bugger off. But she didn't.

"Do you take card?" She asked.

"As it happens, I do."

She excused herself from the bar not long after Diamond returned from the toilets, and hurried to her hotel room. She fell into bed clutching the baggy to her chest, and dreamed of sequins and snowflakes and glitter and trophies.

The next day passed in a whirl of gym exercises, yoga sessions, costume fittings and make-up tests. The evening rolled swiftly around, bringing with it the tech rehearsal. The competing couples had gone over lighting and sound cues with the tech team previously, and this was simply a dry-run for the bodies on the ground.

"First couple will be Pandoka and Gleep," The show runner announced to the congregation of lycra-clad competitors, "Second will be Coagulated Mass B-7 X-9 and Gladys McConnor. Third will be Whisper and Snatch. Fourth will be the android replicas of Torvill and Dean. Fifth, and finally, Stardust and Diamond."

"I still don't know why androids are allowed to compete." Sniffed Gladys McConnor.

"Because it's an all-inclusive competition." Said Diamond, "Plus, you're the one whose partner is a biologically engineered Otherform."

Gladys McConnor turned up her nose.

"We were built to emulate the Original's skills and performance. We have no enhancement or advantage." Said the android replica of Torvil.

"You're simply letting your prejudice show." Said Dean.

The show runner clapped his hands together, "Enough chit-chat folks. First couple on the ice. Pandoka and Gleep, that's you."

Pandoka and Gleep did their run-through. Then Coagulated Mass B-7 X-9 and Gladys McConnor. Then Whisper and Snatch, whose rehearsal had to be paused and restarted when someone hit the wrong button and set off a bunch of pyrotechnics. Then Torvill and Dean.

"Here we go!" Grinned Diamond, "Stardust?" She had vanished. A moment later she returned,

"Sorry. Had to run to the little girl's room."

As they took to the ice, Stardust took a moment to appreciate the rink. It was huge, vast. She hadn't ever skated in one so big in all her career. It was also open-air, if that was the right term for it. The rink was a thin sheet of ice, through which the rocks and boulders and ice crystals of the Ring could be seen tumbling and spinning below. Above, an energy field held in the atmosphere, and the smokey orb of Saturn dominated the view. Beyond that, stars; Countless twinkling flames, dancing in the dark.

Stardust and Diamond skated to their starting positions and waited. While they stood there in the gloom of the unlit rink, with the eerie yellow light reflected from Saturn's clouds glowing over the ice, Stardust felt the pins and needles begin. Her heartbeat raced, and sweat broke out across her forehead and down her spine. Her palms became clammy, and for a moment she felt panic rising in her chest.

"You ok?" Diamond asked, "You don't look well."

"Fine." Stardust said, as the strange sensations subsided, "Absolutely fine." There it was. That calm. That muscular certainty. That uninhibited agility.

"You sure?"

Stardust nodded, and their music started. They went through the motions, as the lights whirred and clicked, and as cameras zoomed and focussed and dollied to and fro at the edge of the rink, and on cranes overhead. The final moves, so tricky for so long, were child's play. Stardust barely felt any fatigue from the gruelling performance. She glanced at Diamond, who was breathing hard and glistening with sweat. She was calm and relaxed. Those pills really were some kind of magic. Her hair had even stayed put.

The show runner thanked all the couples, then scurried off into his burrow of cables and rigging and softly glowing screens.

"Tomorrow's the big day." Said Gleep, her scales glinting like jewels, "Are you excited?"

"Excited to win. That's for sure." Stardust said, smiling.

In her hotel room that night, Stardust lay awake shivering. Her skin was cold to the touch, and no matter how many blankets she wrapped around herself, or how close she sat to the heater, she couldn't get warm. She attempted to make a hot chocolate, but her hands shook so much that she spilled the cocoa powder.

"Damn it." She hissed.

It had started as she felt the effects of the pill wearing off. Perhaps these were the side-effects Ratbag had mentioned. She wished and hoped that they would abate soon, so that she could get a good night's sleep. Hours passed, and Stardust felt worse, not better. Her teeth chattered, and when she looked in the mirror, she cursed.

"I look dreadful." She whined. Her skin was pale, and her eyes bloodshot, "Damn side effects."

But what if they weren't side effects? What if they were a come-down, some kind of withdrawal from the effects of the pills? The one sure way to stop these weird sensations, was obviously to take another pill. She shuffled to the bedside table, where the little baggy sat. Her shaking fingers worked against her, as she tried to pick one. They evaded her fingers at every attempt.

"To hell with this!" She said, lifting the bag, and attempted to dislodge one of the little green items into her mouth. Her shaking hands launched the whole lot down her throat. She coughed and choked, swallowing many more than she intended.

"Shit." She said, when finally she stopped choking and spluttering.

Her heartbeat leapt up a gear, pounding suddenly in her chest, trying to break free. Her stomach cramped, and she doubled over, crying out in pain. Heat flushed through her, and for one moment she thought she might actually burst into flames. Her skin was bright red, throbbing with heat. She fell onto her hands and knees on the floor, unable to hold her own weight as pins and needles sliced through her muscles. She tried to scream, tried to cry out, but she couldn't. Her throat constricted, and her eyes bulged.

She woke up to her alarm chirping 7am. Her eyes snapped open, taking in a strange view. She was staring at the underside of the bed. Slowly, carefully, she picked herself up off the floor. She felt incredibly calm, despite how she had suffered the night before. She could feel the miraculous physical confidence the pills bestowed. Looking at herself in the mirror, she liked what she saw. Her skin was radiant, her hair gorgeously curly and bouncy. She was well-rested, and she breathed deeply.

"Good morning, Abigail Stardust," She said to her reflection, "It's time to become a winner."

*

The rink-side seats were full. Row upon row of people, thousands of them, sat excitedly cheering and chatting, waiting for the spectacle to begin. The presenters were doing a good job of filling the time, waiting for the crew to prep, and for competitors to struggle into their skin-tight sequined costumes. Glitter was liberally applied to every competitor, and to most surfaces. Everything dazzled.

"You're all performing in the same order as tech rehearsal." Reminded the show runner, "Half an hour, then I need you all in the wings ready. Okay?"

The performers nodded, gave thumbs up, and generally responded in the affirmative from their corners of the vast changing room. Sequins and feathers and glitter and spandex hung everywhere.

"You seem unusually quiet." Diamond said, as he pulled his sequined outfit up over his shoulders, "Zip me up?"

Stardust did as asked, "I'm just focussed, I suppose." In truth, she had found it difficult to know how to behave. Her thoughts were elsewhere. It was almost like daydreaming, except the day was real, "Focussed on success."

He smiled at her reassuringly, then rearranged his goolies to a more comfortable position in the figure-hugging outfit, "You're worrying, aren't you? You needn't. You're going to be amazing!"

"I already am amazing." She said, pulling her hair back and fastening it into a bun on the top of her head.

He chuckled at her, and looked around the room, "They're all really good. It could be any of us up there on the winners podium, later."

She gripped his arm, tightly, "No. It will be me."

"Alright, calm down." He said, pulling away from her vice-like grip.

She smiled at him. It was a smile Diamond did not like the look of.

The performers took to the ice, couple by couple. The table of judges gave respectable scores at the end of each performance, which would be tallied with viewer votes at the climax, to calculate the winners.

"That was Pandoka and Gleep," The television announcer said in the break between performances, "They came to Earth as refugees following the Hive wars, and have made quite a name for themselves as ice skaters in very short shrift. Being reptilian, of course, the cool of the rink doesn't suit them very well. But wow, still, what a show they put on for us!"

Coagulated Mass B-7 X-9 and Gladys McConnor's performance wowed the crowd.

"It really is handy having an extra set of legs," Chuckled the announcer, "And Gladys McConnor really knows how to put on a show!"

Whisper and Snatch's performance was slow and balletic, set to down-tempo music, and while very well performed was, as the announcer phrased it, "A perfect point at which to pop the kettle on, while you're waiting for the final, more exciting competitors to take to the ice."

The android replicas of Torvill and Dean spent lots of time in the air, leaping and jumping and twirling.

"Show offs." Gladys hissed in the wings.

"Epitome of a class act." Said the announcer.

"You ready?" Asked Diamond.

Stardust nodded.

They took to the ice under the harsh glare of a silver spotlight. They shone in the darkness like precious gems, as they took a slow turn about the rink, in the dark, in the hush, finding their starting marks. Saturn's great cataracted eye stared blindly down as they began their performance. The music started, slow and ominous, and began to build. Instrument layered upon instrument, and the tempo edged imperceptibly faster and faster. Diamond lifted Stardust and they span. They swept away and together, away and together in vast spirals, showering ice crystals from the blades on their feet as they zigged and zagged over the glass-like rink. The crowd became more and more enthusiastic as the pace intensified, and the leaps and twirls more frequent and frenzied.

"They make it look so effortless, don't they?" Said the television announcer.

Stardust felt her arms and legs moving as if by themselves. Each muscle knew where it had to be, what it had to do, without her having to process any information. She coasted along in her own mind, simply along for the ride. Diamond spun into position for the final move. That tricky move that had caused them so much bother. Stardust was already on her way, poised, perfect. She leaped, and he caught her, and together they spun the full 360, cartwheeling, arms and legs as spokes, into the final leap, and - yes - the graceful landing.

Applause and cheering erupted like fireworks around the rink. The crowd were leaping to their feet, clapping, whooping, cheering, whistling.

Diamond panted, "We did it!" He beamed at Stardust.

Something wasn't right. She was grinning, but there was nothing behind her eyes. She didn't seem to be breathing. She stood rigid and still like a statue.

"Stardust?" Diamond took her hand, squeezed it.

It felt wrong; too boney. Her skin shifted oddly under the pressure of his touch, "Abigail?"

The crowd began to notice something wrong, and the cheering merged with a wave of worried muttering as Stardust buckled at the knees, and collapsed onto the ice. Diamond tried to catch her, but wasn't fast enough. She hit the ice hard and split open a knee. The tear in her skin didn't bleed. It hung open, and underneath wasn't a red wound, but shining green. Diamond looked at the face of his dance partner, a woman he had trained with and been friends with for a decade, and no longer recognised her face. The proportions were off, like looking at a funfair mirror reflection of her. He became vaguely aware of medics rushing towards them from the distant edge of the rink.

"Can you talk?" He asked, "What's the matter?"

He took hold of her hands and tried to pull her up, to stand. Her skin slipped off like gloves. Her hands were green and had too many joints. They trembled, and for the first time she appeared to become aware of her surroundings.

"Did I do it?" She asked, "Did I win?"

Diamond didn't know how to reply. He dropped the skin gloves onto the ice, and stepped away, shaking his head. The medics arrived and hoisted her onto a stretcher, and as they did so, her skin tore and shifted on her form like loose fabric. Her face tore open, and a bulging mirrorball eye erupted out, capped by a twitching insect antenna.

*

Nurses and doctors had fussed over Abigail Stardust for a full two days before Alasdair Diamond was allowed into the private room to see her. She had been squirrelled away into a secure military hospital, scanned, probed, questioned, and examined.

He sat in the single plastic chair near the bed. It was not comfortable at all. Around his friend were all manner of devices, hooked up to her with electrodes, and pipes, and strange metal appendages.

"Stardust? Can you hear me?"

A nurse entered the room and began examining the charts hung on the foot of the bed.

"She's been unresponsive since she came to us." She said, somewhat bluntly.

"What happened to her?" He asked, "What did this to her?" His eyes wavered over her new form, naked on the bed, "She looks like a grasshopper."

The nurse nodded, "It's something called Genetic Tag Enhancement. A new form of performance enhancement."

"I don't understand."

"She was grafting tiny bits of foreign DNA into herself to boost her performance. But something went wrong. Looks to me like an overdose."

"I've never heard anything like that before!"

"It's very new."

"And all those tiny bits of DNA..." Diamond's brain did a somersault as he tried to understand,

"They what, took over?"

The nurse nodded, and left the room.

After a long while sitting and staring at his friend, Diamond edged the chair closer, until he was near enough to reach out and touch her hand. He didn't want to, but it felt the right thing to do.

"Why did you do this to yourself?" He asked quietly.

"To win." Came the reply, in an eerie, faraway voice, "To prove them wrong. To succeed one last time."

"Well we won." Diamond said.

Stardust, or rather, what Stardust had become, sat up and reached out for Diamond. She struggled with the proportions and joints of her new body, and collapsed out of the bed, pulling some of the machines clattering down around her. Diamond knelt and held her, as she looked up at him with those huge glittering eyes.

"We won!" She exclaimed, "I did it!"

She made a strange strangled sound in the back of her throat, and Diamond realised she was crying. He didn't have the heart to also tell her they had been disqualified due to her doping. He let her have her win.

The Venusian Fly Trap

THWACK THWACK THWACK!

His machete hacked at the tangled blue undergrowth, and he grunted with the exertion of every thrust. Rain water splashed off my helmet, ran over my - mostly - waterproof uniform, and filled my boots. For yet another entire Earth-standard day our small party had trudged, achingly slowly, through the near impregnable interior. There had been more of us at the start of the expedition, but only four remained.

"Damned thing's getting blunt." Grunted the unshaven Henry Rose, Captain of the expedition and wielder of the machete. He continued to slash and hack at the vines, thick as an elephant's trunk, but now with less gusto. He wasn't a young man, and the rigours of the last month were taking their toll.

"Perhaps we should stop and make camp here?" Suggested the cartographer, a man known as 'Porky'. His surname, Porcelain, was too dainty a descriptor for someone so brutalist in build.

Rose and Porky did not get on.

"We have a ways yet to go, and are making sinfully little progress!" Rose brandished his blade, "This bally jungle is set against us! We must make haste!"

Leaning back against the blue-grey trunk of a tree, Porky sighed, wiping the incessant rain from his face, "At least let's rest a while. We can push on fortified by a little to drink and some rations, yes?" He looked to me and the final member of the party for backup.

"Porky's right, Captain." I wheezed. My asthma was playing merry hell in the steaming heat of the jungle. I was the party's zoologist, and the youngest by at least a decade. I had been so bright-eyed and eager at blast-off, and now wanted nothing more than to be at home with my cloned Lemurs and android Dodos; Dr Amy Sash. That's me.

"I am rather parched." Announced the final member of the party, a busty, no-nonsense military woman with more medals than she cared to admit. She was on this expedition at the behest of one of Earth's shady and vaguely threatening government agencies, and made Rose often feel distinctly inadequate; Maladie Peal.

The gruff old Captain lowered his hacking arm, and sheathed the blade, "Fine. But only an hour's respite. We have to make up for lost time, as well you all know."

Porky unloaded himself of his engorged backpack, and pulled from a pocket a sheet of tarpaulin. Using elasticated ties, we tethered it as a makeshift roof between the branches of four trees. The rain was temporarily stopped from drenching us, but the percussion of rain on plastic made conversation near impossible. This rainforest lived up to the name. It poured constantly from the dense clouds that made up the Venusian sky. All the while, the uncomfortable heat made the forest floor steam; filling the space between leaves with coils of evaporating water.

"If I'm not drenched by the rain falling down, I'm made clammy by the stuff on its way back up again." Peal said, pulling at her stiff collar, "I've never been so constantly moist. Even my nipples have gone all prune-like."

I pulled a face, but said nothing, instead biting into the brittle brown ration bar. It was said to contain all the vital nutrients for survival. Shame it contained none of the flavour.

"I'd give anything for an apple, or a pear." I said, staring at the unappealing ration, "I think I've forgotten what real food tastes like."

"Say again?" Peal leaned towards me, to better hear what I had said.

"I said I've forgotten what real food tastes like." I repeated loudly in her ear.

Guffawing, Peal slapped a meaty hand on my knee, knocking the ration onto the ground, "This is nothing! I've spent years at a time on deep-space deployment with only those ration bars and recycled water. You'll get used to it."

I didn't want to get used to it, "If only Professor Bounty hadn't... you know. He'd be able to tell us what's edible here, and what isn't." I nudged the wet ration bar with my foot. I was hungry - but it belonged to the floor now.

"Yes, well, he's not here, is he? So we make do."

The Professor had been our botanist. One of the many others in the party who were no longer present. Where they had gone, none of us knew. The Captain and Porky had argued over whether they'd simply wandered off and become lost, or something ... else. I tried not to pay too much attention to what the 'something else' might have been.

I busied myself each day with my study of the animal life that I could find, which was surprisingly little. There was the usual range of pollinating insects, burrowing beetles, and so on, but in much smaller numbers than a dense jungle like this should have been able to maintain. There were fewer birds, if it was at all accurate to use Earthly taxonomic groupings to describe them. Which it likely wasn't. Fewer still larger predators. I'd identified something vaguely cat-like that climbed in a chimpanzee fashion in the upper canopy, and never seemed to venture toward the ground.

As I sat ignoring yet another argument between Rose and Porky that set Peal howling with laughter, I peered beyond the tarpaulin. Was that something moving in the trees? Snatching up my binoculars I fiddled with the focus, peering into the misty blue depths of the forest. There! The cat-ape thing, sheltering under a large leaf as an Englishman does beneath an umbrella. To my surprise it was joined by another, and another. They pointed at us.

They pointed at us!

"I think we're being followed." I said, which none of the others heard. They always insisted on being ever so cacophonous. I made a few notes in my journal, then returned my eyes to the binoculars. The creatures had gone. But something else caught my eye. Movement in the undergrowth. Without thinking, I moved off to investigate. My curiosity was always a dangerously powerful force upon me. It drew me into the torrential rain, towards the movement. I hadn't seen any large predators in the long long time we had been on Venus, and so didn't fear that anything would jump out at me with gnashing teeth or scything claws. Large leaves swayed, as if someone brushed past. Yet I couldn't see anyone. I blamed the downpour for obscuring my vision.

"Hello?" I called into the undergrowth, not entirely sure why.

I paused, as a familiar shape sat up from the leaf litter.

"Professor Bounty?" I was relieved at the sight of him. But the relief was brief. He sat oddly in mulch and brambles. Something was wrong, "Are you unwell?"

The Professor's head swung awkwardly towards me. I gasped. His mouth hung open, and his eyes were clouded. His skin was grey, and marked with luminous blue veins. Lurching forward, he extended a broken arm toward me, and his jaw moved up and down in a parody of speech. There was nothing of him below the waist. Tattered entrails hung like wet leather from inside his rib cage, where a collection of blue vines wound into him.

I stumbled backwards from the grim spectre. The corpse of the Professor seemed to beckon me towards it, and it lurched at me jerkily, a few feet at a time.

The vines.

The vines that grew into his open wound were using him as a puppet!

I screamed, and ran for my life. I tripped and slipped back the way I had come, crying out desperately for Rose, Porky and Peal. I heard them shouting my name, and followed the sound of their voices. I had to stop, unable to fill my lungs. Where was my inhaler? I must have dropped it! Panic rose in my chest, hot and tight as I struggled for breath.

Peal's hands found me and shook me, "What's the matter, girl?" She demanded.

I couldn't speak. I couldn't breathe. I pointed off into the jungle, my eyes wide with fright. Peal dashed off in the direction I had indicated. Rose came by next, and handed me a spare inhaler. I pulled on it urgently, and felt the cool expansion ease my terror. My lungs opened up and I could breathe. I found my voice.

"It's the Professor–" I said, but was cut short by a series of gunshots. Peal had let loose a spray of bullets. I heard them thud into wood and soft soil, "He's dead." I said.

Peal returned a moment later, ashen and pinched, "This way. On the double."

She pushed Rose and me ahead of her, checking over her shoulder regularly.

*

I tried to explain to them what I had seen. Rose and Porky thought I was being a 'flighty woman'. The Captain's words, which he soon took back after a verbal ear-bashing from Peal. She wasn't easily rattled, but the sight of a puppet cadaver was a macabre horror she hadn't been trained to deal with.

"Hungry Mantids, belligerent Thangoreens, even the shape-shifting Graaaks - I've gone up against the worst of the worst!" She said as we marched on, "I've never seen anything of the kind before."

"Pfft." Porky rolled his eyes, "There's no way a plant could do what you describe."

Those were his last words. A vine curled on the ground tightened around his ankle as he stepped by it. He paused and looked down, then vanished. He was dragged off into the steaming foliage. I cried out in surprise, and we all froze.

"Look where you're stepping!" I said, "It's laying traps for us!"

Rose hefted his machete, and ground his teeth together, "No damnable shrub is going to get me!"

THWACK! THWACK!

As his arm came forward for another strike, he too stepped into a coiled vine. It snapped up like teeth upon his leg, and he bellowed in pain. Striking at the constricting blue limb with his blade caused nothing but small nicks. Peal unholstered her gun and fired a shot at the vine. The bullet passed through, leaving a blasted open wound, which sprayed indigo sap into the air. It covered all three of us. The vine went limp.

Wincing, Rose pulled at the twisted woody creeper. His flesh had been punctured by savage thorns. As he unplugged each hole, his blood spread faster, staining his trouser leg.

A dreadful thought occurred to me. "Porky had the map, and the compass."

Peal and Rose stared at me, as they came to the same understanding. Without our cartographer we were very very lost.

"Now what?" I ask.

Peal has already torn open her backpack and begun to tightly bandage Rose's leg, "Lean on me for support, old fella. I don't recommend walking on that leg for a while. Looks a nasty bite."

Since when did a plant bite?

*

The going was slow as I led the way, treading carefully, ducking away from suspiciously neck-high thorny branches. I hated to admit it, but Rose didn't look well. His face was pale, and his breathing seemed laboured. I exchanged a look with Peal, and it was clear she shared my concerns. But what were we to do? Our options were limited.

The decision was made to head in the direction we had been travelling in for as long as we could. We appeared to be going uphill, and so would soon reach high ground, and be able to get a good view of the landscape and its layout. If we made camp in a place like that, when the return ship came to pick us up, we could more easily see it, and get its attention.

That was the plan.

We stopped for a rest, sheltering from the rain under broad leaves as best we could, with the tarpaulin having been snatched away with Porky.

Rose coughed wetly, and a spray of yellow oil erupted from his lips. I jumped up, as his eyes bulged, and he clutched his chest.

"Rose, old boy?" Peal said, her hand going instinctively for her weapon, "What is it?"

The Captain spluttered and choked, as something emerged from his mouth, filling his airways. It was a blue shoot. A curling frond, opening up more rapidly than I could imagine, blossoming into a brilliant spray of greenish-blue oval leaves. Rose twitched and died, as the plant's roots erupted from the wounds in his leg, falling limp on the soil.

Peal swore, and I was numb. I'd never seen anyone die before. And this was a horrible, agonising, confusing death. I wouldn't wish it on anyone. Its emergence complete, the plant seemed to rest, gently fanning its leaves in the rain.

*

We had to keep on. There was no point dawdling. There was no point trying to explain it, or understand it. From the corner of my eye, every movement was now a malevolent creeper coming to use me as compost for its saplings. Peal marched in the lead now, with her gun in one hand, and Rose's machete in the other. We climbed a steep incline, up and up and up we went. The rain stopped, and a mist rolled in around us.

We were in the clouds. We continued up, and found ourselves in a rocky mountain-top clearing. The clouds hung below us, thick and turquoise and violently roiling. The sky above us was a pale purple dome, sprinkled with a few stars. The air was thin here, but it was a relief to breath air that wasn't saturated with water.

"Look at this." Peal said, pointing with the blade. It seemed to be a web. An overlapping, fleshy web of vines. Some were thorny, others bore the same oval leaves that had erupted from Rose's mouth. They all of them seemed to emerge from a crack in the rock; A crevice, a cave, a lair.

I moved towards it; Curiosity once more making a fool of me. I grabbed at my mouth to stifle a squeak of fear. The vines at the cave mouth flexed and moved. They were wound around something large, pink, and wearing a back-pack. Porky's partly-digested body appeared to be melting away under the pressure of the plant around it, some strange chemical reaction to an oil the plant was exuding.

"Help me!"

Porky was still alive! Somehow, he lived!

Without a word, Peal shot the man between the eyes. I screamed as his head erupted open, and bits of skull and brain splattered the ground.

"Let's get away from here." Peal said.

I couldn't keep my eyes from the grotesque Jackson Pollock spread over the exposed rock.

"He asked for our help!" I said, my voice small.

"That was the only help we could offer." Peal was hard as flint, her stare could light sparks. I didn't protest further.

"Something's coming." I said.

I could feel it through my waterlogged boots; an approaching tremble below the soil. It was growing in strength, and was definitely not a quake. I backed up from the cave mouth just in time as a huge set of snapping jaws burst out and clamped down. A second's delay and it would have been my head in those jaws. They snapped and snapped at thin air. I launched back, falling over its web of flexing roots and vines. Leaves quivered as I hurried by, towards the sturdy form of Peal.

I grabbed at her, "Quickly! We have to go! We can't stay here!"

But the sturdy woman wouldn't budge. She stared at the plant, snapping it's enormous fleshy jaws from the crooked cave mouth, then sagged to her knees, and blood began to flow from her mouth. A thorny vine had pierced her through the spine, and had begun to push its way into her.

I didn't know what to do. I had nowhere to run. My lungs were burning. The thrashing blue and green plant rose up, undulating and convulsing all around me, closing in. Those jaws, snap, snap, snapping closer and closer as it pulled it's hulking form across the mountaintop.

With a yodelling wail, my vision was filled with furry bodies. Lithe bodies, with tails and claws and glinting yellow eyes. They came bounding out of nowhere, tumbling and spinning like acrobats. The cat-ape creatures! They took me up and carried me off.

*

I must have passed out, as when I woke, I was far from the mountain, in some kind of fortified tree-top nest. These are no primitive beasts. They are primitive, yes. But intelligent. They live in woven homes, suspended in great clusters in the canopy. There they are shielded from view by the foliage, and protected from the hungry vines and creepers that feed that great mountaintop maw.

Last week I watched the return craft come and, after a futile wait, go again. I'm lost. But I'm not alone. These cat-ape people have taken me in.

The natural hierarchy of this world is topsy-turvy, and if I can learn enough about it - hopefully I can weed this garden ahead of any future missions from Earth. Hopefully one day, if someone Human finds this journal, they will be warned of the vicious flora of

Venus, before they are dragged screaming into its compost heap.

Farewell Tour

"Nancy Crepe, the biggest rock star of his generation, died on stage, shot in the chest by person or persons unknown. At least, that is what everyone believed." The host of the TV show was a wide-set man in his late 50s with a shock of white hair. He had the attitude of a hard-bitten copper who'd seen a few crazy things in his career. He hadn't. But the producers had a particular look in mind for the host when they opened up auditions; and he fit the bill, "Let's go back to the beginning of the Farewell Tour, and examine what we know to have taken place. What you will see tonight are reenactments, and portions of interviews, where significant, with the people involved in this truly bizarre case..."

CROSS FADE TO: INTERIOR TOUR BUS, OUTER SPACE.

"It's a 79-date tour. Your farewell tour. Once it's done, you can retire."

"Pfft!" Nancy scoffed, rolling his eyes, "A rock 'n' roller shouldn't retire. He should go out in a blaze of glory, power-sliding into the great bleak oblivion beyond!"

The stiffly-suited manager was at his wits end.

CUT TO: MEDIUM CLOSE UP. INTERVIEW, ROBOLD SPOON.

The manager's head and shoulders appeared on-screen, much older than the reenactment's actor.

"Nancy and the Pants had been one of the biggest rock bands of the age," He said, "Leather-clad, studded, ripped jeans and spiked hair, thrusting loudly on stage, sending massed audiences into states of near-delirium. The usual rock and roll punk thing of the time. They were the first, caught the zeitgeist and rode it to stardom."

CUT TO: INTERIOR, TOUR BUS. OUTER SPACE.

The band members slouched around the tour bus in various states of geriatric discomfort. The band consisted of Nancy the vocalist, Y-Fronts the bassist. Boxer on lead guitar and Jock Strap on drums. There had been a couple more at the start; but Commando and Brief quit the band before they made it big.

"But all of Jupiter's moons? Really?" Nancy asked, "It's a bit heavy, man."

"Each venue has sold out. You can't back out now. You agreed to it already. You signed the contracts!"

Robold swayed as the tour bus rattled onward. He had been their manager since his father passed away, who was their manager before him - and knew exactly how difficult these ageing rockers could be.

Nancy sat eye-balling him in old grey pyjamas and a leather jacket covered in patches, swigging something noxious from his hip flask, "I signed no such thing."

"I think I remember signing it." Jock Strap muttered from his bunk, adjusting his toupee, "Pass me that Chit-Chat magazine. I want to have a go at the crossword."

Robold sighed, "It's too late to argue about it anyway. You've already done the first gig, so there's only 78 to go."

"We've done one already?" Y-Fronts sat up suddenly, eyes boggling.

"It's all groovy, Y-Fronts. You were, am, and is astronomical." Nancy soothed his band mate, whose mind was somewhat addled by a youth of hard drink, harder drugs, and back-alley genetic manipulation.

"Do you know where you are?" Nancy asked.

Y-Fronts looked about slowly. Seeing the vast red storms of Jupiter through the windows he ventured, "Cardiff?"

Robold sighed, he was fed up and needed a good night's sleep; something he was unlikely to get any time soon, "You're on the tour bus."

Y-Fronts nodded slowly, "Wake me when we get to Liverpool" Then he fell asleep.

"Is he ok?" Robold asked, "I know the doctors said he was physically well enough to do the tour, but, well..."

Nancy shrugged, "So long as he doesn't forget how to play the songs, he can be anywhere he wants in there," He tapped the side of his own head, "Venturing into a technicolour dream-scape to the sound of slap-bass and bongos."

Pausing his crossword to readjust his toupee, Jock Strap asked, "Where did we gig last night?"

"Adrastea."

"And tonight?"

"Aitne."

"And tomorrow?"

"Amalthea."

"Don't tell me you booked them in alphabetical order?" Jock Strap tutted, turning his attention back to the crossword, "Numbskull!" He said loudly, jotting the word in 5-down.

A few quiet minutes passed, before Nancy spoke again, "Anything worth reading in the way of reviews?"

"Only the usual." Robold said, "Nothing worth framing."

Nancy had a perverse love for bad reviews. The worst of the worst he framed, and hung on the walls around his house. Amongst his favourites were the scathing reviews that variously described his music as the sound of 'chaos set to a 4:4 beat', 'shouting with drums', and 'very bad'.

Nodding, Nancy wriggled into the depths of his chair, "Let me know when it's time to sound check."

CUT TO: MEDIUM CLOSE UP, INTERVIEW, JOCK STRAP

Jock Strap's mechanical apparatus filled the square tv screen. He was little more than a head and torso now, connected to vats of bubbling liquid, machines that went ping now and then, pumps, gizmos, doo-hickies, and suchlike that kept him alive long past his expected expiration date. His infamous toupee still rested awkwardly on his barren dome.

"The Aitne gig went well." His voice hummed electronically from a black box fitted to his throat, "We only blew out two speakers, and Nancy only forgot the words to one song. But he knew how to handle that situation; hold the mic out at the crowd and let them sing the song until he remembered the next line. The crowd loved that shit! They felt involved and a part of the show. Plus it gave Nancy a minute to catch his breath."

CUT TO: INTERIOR ARENA. FINALE OF CONCERT.

The final song played, they took their bows, and then the rigging collapsed. Luckily, none of the band were on their marks, else there would have been one hell of a mess, and no encore. The chaotic group were all over the stage, and just went with it. Sparks showered everywhere, metal clanged against metal, and they held up their hands and gave 'heavy metal fingers' to the crowd, who cheered the spectacle, not knowing how close the band had come to playing their final concert.

CUT TO: MEDIUM CLOSE UP. INTERVIEW, ROBOLD SPOON.

"No, at first we had no idea it hadn't been an accident." The aged Robold held up his hands, "To be honest, the guys thought it was all a part of the spectacle of the finale that they'd forgotten was planned. But we soon found out that someone had it in for us."

CUT TO: INTERIOR, HOTEL SUITE.

The next day brought a review that Nancy adored. He tore it from the paper and waved it about proudly, howling with laughter, "Listen to this, 'I almost wish the band had been taken out by the collapsing set, then no other right-thinking person would be made to suffer through a Nancy gig'. Now that'd be a Rock and Roll way to go."

Robold took his phone from his ear and jabbed the red button to end the call, "I've some bad news." The band looked at him, curious, "The incident last night..."

"Which was spectacular!" Jock Strap grinned, peering out of the bathroom door, where he was washing his toupee in the sink.

"...Was not an accident." Robold pinched the bridge of his nose, "I can't believe I'm going to ask this, but do you have any enemies that would go to the trouble of sabotaging you, or maybe even attempting to kill you?"

Boxer, the usually silent and thoughtful member of the group started counting on his fingers, "Craggy Geoff, Three-Finger Margaret, Kasselfesselfine, Rid The Pog, Heavy-Handed Jake, Dreadre Nose..."

"Ones I'm not already aware of?" Robold interrupted.

Boxer shook his wide head, "Nope. You know about all my nemesisisis."

Nancy shrugged, "I don't recall any new ones that need adding to the list. But give me a week and I'm sure I can bag a few more." He winked.

"Please don't." Robold said.

CUT TO: MEDIUM CLOSE UP. INTERVIEW, JOCK STRAP.

He laughed; a gargled buzzing sound, "Yeah, we had all lived quite colourful lives. Pissed off enough people to make us infamous as well as famous."

CUT TO: MEDIUM CLOSE UP. INTERVIEW, ROBOLD SPOON.

Robold pinched the bridge of his nose, "Nancy wanted to see the stage. He wanted to see how it had come crashing down. He was like that. If there was a car accident, he'd be the one to demand the tour bus slow down so he could see what had happened. Morbid curiosity."

CUT TO: INTERIOR ARENA.

"The supports were partially cut, and primed with small explosives, to go off at a certain time, and bring the whole lot down." Said the grey-faced stage manager, who had clearly not had a wink of sleep.

Police were still crawling over the stage and wings, and people in high-vis and hard hats were beginning to crane the wreckage off the stage.

"Far out." Nancy said.

Once the stage was clear and deemed safe, Nancy and Robold made their way into the open space. They patrolled the scene, and Nancy couldn't help but whistle a jaunty tune. It seemed to offset the mood of the place nicely; all shock and gloom. From high up in the remains of the gantries and rigging that criss-crossed the stage, a piece of paper fluttered down. Nancy plucked it out of the air, and chuckled at it. But only for a moment. He grew serious, and tucked away the paper before Robold could catch a glimpse.

"Impressive job." Nancy said, "So when do we make tracks for the next performancipation?"

Robold checked his watch, "Half an hour ago. Come on, we're late.

CUT TO: MEDIUM CLOSE UP. INTERVIEW, ROBOLD SPOON.

"I don't know why he didn't show me the flyer. He'd known me my whole life. I'd hoped he would have trusted me." The aged Robold shrugged, sunk low in his chair.

CUT TO: INTERIOR, TOUR BUS. OUTER SPACE.

The cramped craft rattled and swerved towards the next destination as Nancy showed the other members of the band what he had found.

"A flyer?" Jock Strap cocked an eyebrow.

"Not just any old piece of advertisement. One of ours!"

He waved it in their faces. It was from their very first tour, before Commando and Brief left the band. Before they got big. It advertised their debut album 'Together Until The End'. Only the first two words had been scribbled over.

"Ominous." Jock Strap shouted, grabbing up his cross word and jotting the word in 10 across.

"Should we show the coppers?" Boxer asked, "Or Robold?"

Nancy shook his head, "Negative, my friend. Once the tour is over we'll pay a little visitation upon our erstwhile band mates, and severely chide them for such heavy activities."

The four of them nodded in agreement.

CUT TO: MEDIUM CLOSE UP. INTERVIEW, JOCK STRAP.

The mechanisms of life wheezed and glugged.

"We hadn't spoken to Commando or Brief since they left the band. It hadn't been an entirely friendly parting of ways. Bad blood. They resented our success, and the way Robold - Robold Senior that is, not Robold Junior - had taken pains to write their share of royalties out of the equation, as each new contract and album came around. They were left with nothing. We didn't know this until it was too late.

CUT TO: MEDIUM CLOSE UP. INTERVIEW, ROBOLD SPOON.

"My dad was cut-throat." Robold said sadly, "More so that I ever knew. It all came out at the inquest after Nancy's death. I was mortified."

CUT TO: MONTAGE: GIGS AT VARIOUS ARENAS AND STADIUMS.

A week of rowdy gigs progressed in a dizzying haze of hard liquor, octogenarian groupies, and copy-and-paste stadiums. They went as well as can be expected, which is never 'well', but at least, Robold thought happily, there had been no more deliberate tampering with the set.

The group of bureaucrats that imposed law and order on the moons of Jupiter began an investigation into the sabotage, but worked painfully slowly, and communicated even less efficiently than the band did.

CUT TO: WIDE SHOT, STUDIO.

The host of the show walked slowly across the set, done up like a forensics lab, talking to camera as he went, "All the while, Nancy kept that flyer in his pocket, and with each passing day he grew more and more angry at the suggestion it posed; That his former bandmates, people he had considered good friends, would want to kill him. He likely thought about many forms of revenge. Perhaps pouring hot wax in their eyes. Maybe stapling their fingers to their toes. Beatings. Poisonings. Flinging hot dog poop at them? Until eventually, he might have had a lightbulb moment.

CUT TO: INTERIOR, TOUR BUS. OUTER SPACE.

"Far out." Nancy said, grinning, "Two birdies, one proverbial."

CUT TO: MONTAGE: GIGS AT VARIOUS ARENAS AND STADIUMS.

And the tour ticked on. Callisto. Carme. Carpo. Chaldene. It was around here that Jock Strap finished the crossword, and began another. Cyllene was the next stop, and as the tour bus rattled into the space-dock, Nancy grinned a determined grin.

CUT TO: INTERIOR, TOUR BUS. DOCKED.

"Tonight's going to be a good gig. I can feel it." Robold said. He said it whenever they arrived somewhere new.

"Surely, it will be unlike any other." Nancy smirked.

"What? What was that?"

"Nothing, my friend, nothing at all." And he sauntered off the bus, shouldering his tatty backpack of toiletries and underwear. It seemed heavier today than normal, and Robold eyed the front man suspiciously.

"Do you think he's been weird lately?" Robold asked Y-Fronts, who stared back at him blankly, "I'm asking the wrong person. Never mind."

"Ok." Y-Fronts said, as one of his eyes wandered off to the left.

In their various ramshackle ways, the band members disembarked the cramped tour bus, and were led into the glass-domed city that clung like a barnacle to the tiny moon Cyllene. They were shown to their hotel, and then swiftly escorted to the venue; a smaller arena than some of the others, but the arched windows in the ceiling gave an impressive view of Jupiter's engorged belly.

CUT TO: MEDIUM CLOSE UP. INTERVIEW, ROBOLD SPOON.

"He was always a private man." Robold said of Nancy, "But there were certain things that tipped me off there was something going on. He always sipped from that horrible hip flask. He was always on the edge of tiddled. But he'd stopped swigging. He was talking less. He wasn't engaging with the band as much. If I'd known then what I know now... well, we likely wouldn't be making this show would we?"

CUT TO: GIG VENUE, PRE CONCERT.

Nancy arrived late, later even than he was usually prone to being, and the sound check had already begun. Jock Strap was dishing out a smooth jazz beat on the drums, as Y-Fronts noodled on his bass guitar, the head of which was bristling with untamed strings.

"Here he is." Robold sighed, "Better late than never."

"I honour you with my presence." The front man smirked at his manager, as he sauntered up onto the stage.

As the sound engineers had them go through various combinations, testing levels and mixes and setting the lighting just-so, Nancy seemed unusually calm. He didn't once sip from his noxious hip flask.

'He's up to something.' Robold thought, watching the old man closely. He had been around these rockers his whole life, and knew when things were amiss.

Boxer snapped his D string, and so everything paused while he restrung and re-tuned his guitar. In this brief gap, Nancy vanished into the shadows of the wings, towards a series of dressing rooms and cupboards that hid there. Robold excused himself from his seat beside the sound desk, and followed Nancy. No one paid much attention to him as he climbed onto the stage and drifted, as nonchalantly as he could manage - which wasn't very nonchalant at all - into the darkness. The doors of the various dressing rooms and cupboards were all painted black. All the better to hide them in the dark. Robold moved from one to another, listening at the doors. Nothing.

Nothing. Nothing. At the fourth door, he heard shuffling, and moved back from the door in time to not be hit in the face as it opened. Nancy stepped out and stopped, clocking Robold loitering nearby.

"What are you up to?" He asked.

"I could ask you quite a similar thing." Nancy said.

"Nancy," Robold sighed, "I can tell when something's up. You're acting strange. What's going on?"

CUT TO: MEDIUM CLOSE UP. INTERVIEW, ROBOLD SPOON.

"His bravado cracked for a moment. Less than a moment." Robold took his thick spectacles off to clean as he spoke, "The swagger, the puffed-out chest, the cocky half-smirk, they all seemed to glitch and dissipate for an instant." He put his glasses back on, sliding them gently up the bridge of his nose, "Underneath it all I detected the very weary, tired old man he really was. Someone whose contemporaries sat in comfy armchairs drinking sweet tea and watching daytime tv, expecting grandchildren to come and visit; Someone who had never known a quiet life, and whose well-cultivated veneer was beginning to wear thin."

CUT TO: GIG VENUE, BACKSTAGE.

The moment passed, and Nancy wagged a finger at his manager, "Snooping is a bad habit."

"I wasn't... Ok fine, I was snooping. But It's my job to look after you. You're none of you a spring chicken any more, and I want this tour to go well!"

"I'm seventy eight years young, my piquant administrator. You're only worried about the job you won't have when all this is over."

"No."

"Me, I'm not worried. And you needn't fret over me. Now, vamoose, and let me finish this sound check."

And finish it they did.

CUT TO: MEDIUM CLOSE UP. INTERVIEW, JOCK STRAP.

"The hours between the sound check and the gig whizzed by, and the arena filled to bursting." He said in his garbled electronic voice, "The support act was a young four-piece called Filigree Feathers who performed in a new style called 'baroque and roll'; An electric harpsichord, two lutes, and an enthusiastic girl on the tambourine made up the band. Nancy didn't much care for it, but they were the next big thing, and Robold clearly had his sights set on signing them up to his agency."

CUT TO: GIG VENUE, CONCERT COMMENCING.

It was time for Nancy And The Pants to take to the stage. When they did the crowd went wild. Someone threw their knickers on the stage, someone else threw their false teeth. Nancy accepted all these gifts, pocketing them and blowing kisses into the air. They started with one of their middle-of-the-road hits; a warmer-upper. They progressed into the harsher, punkier, dirtier tracks, aiming for a riot of sound just in time for a brief intermission.

CUT TO: WIDE SHOT, STUDIO.

The host held up a clip board, reading from it, "The set list went as follows; 'Hiding From Her Husband In A Closet', 'Hard Liquor, Harder Morning', 'Behead The King, Bed The Queen', 'Kick A Fascist', 'Colonise This', 'I Thought It Was A Dog But It Was A Skunk', and notably, 'Together Until The End'.

CUT TO: GIG VENUE. MID CONCERT.

The final chords of their early hit clashed and thrashed through the crowd, who leaped and whooped and whistled and cheered, clapping and slapping their hands together.

Nancy shaded his eyes from the bright lights, smiling out at the sea of adoring fans, "Thank you. You're all amazing." Then he noticed something way back in the crowd, and his smile fell.

Beside the tech desk, Robold followed Nancy's gaze, but could see nothing other than rigging and lights. What was he looking at?

A gunshot rang out.

Robold leaped out of his skin, covering his head with his hands, as a series of shocked screams leaped from the massed audience. A cold fear gripped him, as he turned back to the stage. Nancy was laid on his back, not moving. Y-Fronts, Boxer, and Jock Strap threw down their instruments and ran to their fallen band mate.

Someone beside Robold said "Close the curtains." and someone else said "There aren't any!" and then Robold said, "Call an ambulance!"

CUT TO: MEDIUM CLOSE UP. INTERVIEW, JOCK STRAP.

The machines wheezed and clicked as Jock Strap took a thoughtful pause, "He went down like a sack of shit." His brow creased, "I didn't see what he saw. The lights were too bright, shining in my eyes. But I saw him looking at something, and then bang, he went down, his t-shirt stained red. The rest is a blur, to be honest.

CUT TO: MEDIUM CLOSE UP. INTERVIEW, ROBOLD SPOON.

"The rest of the guys filled me in amid all the panic and fuss; about the flyer, and their suspicions. I didn't believe it, in all honesty. I was in shock for days." His eyes were red, and the bags under them twitched.

CUT TO: MEDIUM CLOSE UP. INTERVIEW, JOCK STRAP.

"People were running back and forth, medics, tech crew, roadies, then the ambulances arrived. We didn't know what to do; Y-Fronts, Boxer, and me. Dumbstruck, we just kinda hung around. Waiting to be told what to do, I suppose. It was a bit of an unusual situation." He paused, and his machines rattled and wheezed as he suppressed emotion, "They carried him off before the police got there. It could have been in an ambulance. It could have been by some stage hands. It could have been anyone. Everyone was shocked and dazed. But his body was gone no more than five minutes after he was shot."

CUT TO: WIDE SHOT, STUDIO.

"Who had been amongst the lighting?" The host banged a fist onto a balsa wood table that wobbled, "Who was the gunman, who snuffed out the life of the greatest rock and roll front man of the last century? Or, as the conspiracy theorists ask, was there actually a gunman at all? Was he really shot?" He raised one eyebrow and paused for dramatic effect.

CUT TO: MEDIUM TWO SHOT. INTERVIEW COMMANDO & BRIEF (ARCHIVE FOOTAGE)

The two old men sat hunched and scowling, "We had been screwed over. Left for dust by the rest of them. Of course we were bitter." Said Commando.

Brief nodded, "It was my idea, collapsing the rigging. We hadn't meant to off them. But I was never very good with explosives. They were meant to go off before the gig and ruin the start of the tour."

Nodding, Commando said, "Everyone suspected us of his murder. Given our escapades on Aitne I wasn't surprised."

"But it wasn't us." Brief grunted, "Couldn't have been."

"Couldn't have been." Commando agreed, "Because when he was shot we were already in custody for the collapsed rigging debacle."

"Couldn't have a better alibi than that, eh?" Brief grinned venomously.

CUT TO: WIDE SHOT, STUDIO.

"That interview was filmed six years ago, before both Commando and Brief sadly passed away at the ages of ninety seven and ninety four, respectively. The footage has been released to us by their relatives."

The host moved to a stool and sat awkwardly on its edge, "So who did shoot Nancy? Conspiracy theorists will state again and again that Nancy faked his own death, that no one was in the rigging. That it was an elaborate ruse, involving paid-off stage hands and security aiding and abetting the illusion. The reasons were given are multitudinous and range from the believable to the ridiculous. However, most would likely agree that the real reason for this grand deception was an attempt at framing Commando and

Brief, in a misguided act of revenge for their tampering with the set.

CUT TO: MEDIUM CLOSE UP. INTERVIEW, CONCERT ATTENDEE

"I saw him sneak away, you know." Said the wide red-painted lips of a woman in sunglasses, "I was there, at that gig. I happened to be in the right place at the right time, I suppose. There was all this kerfuffle with ambulances trying to get in and out, thousands of people from the gig milling about. But I saw him. I did, honestly. I knew it was him, slipping away in disguise while everyone was distracted. He was in a wide brimmed hat and cloak. I know he clocked me, and we shared a look. He held his finger up to his lips and went 'sshh'. Then he was off like a ferret down a rat-hole, and away. Honest to goodness, that's what happened. He's still out there somewhere, laughing at us all. Or regretting what he did. Either way, he's out there. He's out there. And if he's watching this show, my name is Magatha Wicks, I live on Mercury, Sun-Side of course, and I am his biggest fan! He's welcome to come and visit me anytime. I won't tell anyone. He's safe with me." She licked her lips provocatively at the camera, and giggled.

Something Else

He had left the stars behind. Without their power his sails were limp, and the speed of his ship waned.

Peering aft, he could make out the distant glittering line of the Milky Way; the edge of which he had passed many months ago.

He pulled at the rigging and drew in the sails, for they were useless now. Calculating his speed, and the rate of deceleration, he discovered when exactly his ship would finally lose all solar power, and begin to drift.

Nothing moved in this void of voids; A stillness unknown to science. Turning his eyes forward, he spun the wheel as far as it would go. With a great creaking and straining of ropes and planks, the ship began to pivot. Painfully slowly, he turned his heading back the way he had come.

What had he expected to find beyond the confines of his native galaxy?

Not this. Not nothing.

Something. Something new. Something else...

The Deep

They had been at war so long, in the crushing darkness, that no one alive remembered why they were fighting. And yet fight they did with increasing frequency. Depth-charges would rain down from Those Above, battering the cities and submarines of Those Below. Then up would launch rockets and balloon-bombs, to smash into the bellies of the cities and skimmers and boats of Those Above, fired by Those Below..

"Man the submersibles." Shouted the commodore over the tannoy, as red warning lights flashed.

The officers and able crewmen from the navy of Those Below ran along rattling, clanking metal gang-planks, leaping through narrow hatches, and into the hulking cylinders of their submarine vessels. They were dented and blemished by not only the battles they had endured, but by the very waters through which they sailed; the ice-seas of Uranus. So cold it would kill a man in moments, yet never froze solid.

The powerful engines of the submersibles rattled and choked into black-smoke-belching life and slid, gurgling, into the frigid depths.

Sonar bleeped and pinged in the cramped stillness of the submarine control room. The captain gave orders relating to speed and heading, which were put into action by the seaman at the controls before him. The space was low-ceilinged, dimly lit, and musty. Green light from the various computer screens arranged around the controls mixed with the red lights that signalled battle stations, casting everything into unreal luminous shades.

"The *Stockport* and the *Oldham* are coming alongside, sir." Reported young seaman Bottle, listening to the coded radio chatter of their sister ships through a pair of oversized headphones.

The captain nodded, "Check on the status of the *Cheadle*. Find out why they're dawdling."

"Sir."

The captain moved from one control station to another, peering over the shoulders of the officers and seamen stationed there, "Prime the top-side battery. I want a full spread of balloons ready to go on my mark."

"Sir."

"The *Cheadle* is alongside, sir."

Nodding, the captain returned to his station in the centre of the room, "Relay to the other vessels; attack pattern 'dolphin'. Staggered balloon release."

Seaman Bottle relayed the command to the *Stockport*, *Oldham* and *Cheadle*, positioned alongside. While the captain waited for the 'understood' signals to return, he resisted the urge to pace the floor. He was an old man. Too long in the tooth for much more of this stress. It was high time for some new blood to take command of his battered old tub. The *Didsbury* had done him proud, and survived more battles than most, much like himself.

"Understood, sir. All vessels ready."

The captain nodded, "On my mark, release hell. Mark."

The *Oldham, Stockport, Cheadle* and *Didsbury* began moving away from each other, releasing one explosive balloon after another. They moved gently, in an expanding spiral, then back inward again. The curtain of charged explosives drifted silently upward, disappearing into the dark.

The captain was knocked off his feet. The *Didsbury* bucked like a bad-tempered mule, knocking men into walls, ceilings, and bulkheads. The seamen in the control room, once they had picked themselves up off the floor, began shouting out information; proximity, damage, and more facts and figures were barked and yapped at the captain's ears.

"Was that one of the balloons?" He asked.

"No sir. It wasn't an explosion."

"Then what was it?"

The sonar technician stood up and backed away from his console, "Sir! You'd better take a look at this."

The captain moved to examine the green glowing screen of the radar, and scowled, "What is it?" He asked.

"I don't know sir. But whatever it is, it's huge. And it's coming back!"

The captain grabbed at a pipe fixed to the wall, "Brace for impact!" He bellowed.

Seaman Bottle winced as his headphones were filled with a sudden, screaming static, and he failed to brace in time.

A great clanging rent the air as the metal reverberated under their feet. The submarine was shocked by some huge collision. The sounds of tearing metal and stalling engines drowned out the shouts and cries of the crew, as they were tossed about, as the sub spun and jerked. Lights flickered and failed. Sparks erupted from shorting control consoles, and puffs of acrid smoke filled the close atmosphere. The submarine settled onto it's side, allowing the crew who could, to stand and assess their situation.

The captain felt his ears pop, as the pressure changed.

"We're descending." Said the seaman at the helm.

"Sinking?" The captain asked.

"No sir, we're being dragged." He turned to stare at the captain, eyes wide with fright, "Something has hold of us and is pulling us down!"

*

Something shook seaman Bottle, and he came to in near-darkness. Where was he? His mind was a muddle, and he struggled to piece together his most recent memories. Pushing himself up against the bulkhead beside him, he was able to sit up.

He had been making his way astern. The captain's panicked voice telling all hands to abandon ship. Then everything had gone black. Maybe he had bashed his head as the submarine was shaken violently from side to side once again. He now, using the wall for support, began rising from the floor. He put his hand to the back of his head and felt the warmth of fresh blood. He felt for the wound, and couldn't find anything more than a small scratch. He hoped he didn't have serious concussion.

"Bottle, you're alive!"

Seaman Bottle blinked a couple of times and recognised the figure coming towards him along the narrow passage.

"Manners!" Seaman Bottle gulped and strained his ears, the pressure was higher than it should have been, and was giving him an ache in his inner ear. His bunk-mate approached with a limp.

"I thought you were dead." Manners hugged him, "Are you ok? What happened to you?"

"I don't know." Bottle admitted, "Last thing I heard was the captain's order to abandon ship. Then I must have bashed my noggin. How long have I been unconscious?"

Manners examined Bottle's head wound, "At least fifteen minutes. Some of the crew did get out in the life buoys. But there's a tear in the hull amidships. Don't know if anyone in the engine rooms got out." He paused to gulp, and wet his lips nervously, "I think we're the only ones left."

Bottle felt numb. The prospect of perishing at sea was ever-present for a seaman, but Bottle always imagined his end would be sudden; going up in a ball of bubbling fire from a torpedo blast. Not this. Not being left behind on a sinking sub. His knees buckled, and Manners had to prop him up to stop him falling onto the ground. They stayed silent for a while, neither sure what to say.

"Well, I have to look on the bright side," Manners said eventually, "At least I'm here with you."

They shared a bittersweet smile.

"Can we get to the control room?" Bottle asked, clutching onto Manners for support.

"I was on my way there when I found you. Come along, let's go."

*

The control stations were all dead. Backup batteries powered the meagre lighting, and not much else. Bottle and Manners struggled through the hatch, and paused there. Several bodies lay broken over chairs and across the floor.

"We had a lucky escape." Manners said, indicating their comparatively minor wounds.

Bottle passed from one seaman to the next, until he found the captain, staring milky-eyed at the ceiling. Kneeling down, he gently closed the old man's eyes.

"Is there any way of sending an SOS?" Manners asked, as he punched at the buttons on the comms controls station; Bottle's station. Nothing happened.

The two men examined the controls, twisted dials, flicked switches, and rattled levers. Getting frustrated, Bottle fished out his multi-tool. Every able seaman was expected to carry one at all times. You never knew when you would be the first to find a leak, or a loose bolt, or something else that needed a hurried fix. He used the screwdriver adapter to remove the stiff screws that held the facia panels in place.

"There's a series of interlinked batteries in each station," Bottle said as he worked his hands into the tangled wiring of the station, "If they're not too damaged, I might be able to get enough for a mayday."

Manners moved to the helm, and cast his eyes over the readouts there. These were more analogue and manual than the others, and registered depth, speed, current, and pressure. Among other things.

"This can't be right." Manners breathed, tapping the glass dome of the depth gauge.

"What can't be right?" Bottle was now up to his elbows in his control station's guts.

"We're still descending."

Bottle scowled, "What's our depth?"

"I don't know, that gauge seems broken."

"What does it say?"

"Forty four hundred thousand fathoms... I think?"

Bottle paused, shoulder deep, "But that's the very bottom of the ocean. There's no deeper we can go!"

With a dull clunk, the comms controls came to flickering life. Bottle extracted his arms and pushed the facia plates back into place. Twisting a dial, flicking a switch, and jabbing a big red button, he sunk onto the seat beside him, "The SOS is broadcasting. But I'm not sure anyone will hear it."

"Why not?"

"We're too deep. The ocean is too dense for a signal to travel very far. And that battery won't last forever."

"And some good news, please?" Manners wiped his hands down his face, desperately seeking some glimmer of hope.

The metal beneath their feet shuddered briefly, and the submarine rocked gently too and fro, settling.

"We've stopped descending." Manners said, glancing at the depth gauge.

They waited. What they were waiting for was death. They both knew they were alone, lost in the freezing cold depths, with no way of finding their way back to the flotilla-city they called home. They sat on the floor, their backs against the cold wall. The chill of the ice had begun seeping into the air. Manners could see his breath clouding, more and more with every exhalation. Bottle shuffled in close to him for warmth, and they linked arms, Manners resting his head on his bunk-mate's shoulder.

"Any regrets?" Bottle asked.

"I won't be having any sentimental or morbid talk, thank you very much." Manners said through chattering teeth.

Bottle laughed, and pulled in closer, "I've got one." He said, squirming around so that they were facing each other, limbs twisted together.

"Oh yes?" Manners cocked an eyebrow.

Bottle leaned in and kissed him. Manners kissed him back. They pushed their bodies together; winding arms and legs, and heaving chests. Manners felt Bottle's stiff attention pressing into his thigh, and pushed his own meaty salute forward. Hands undid trousers, grabbing at hot flesh, gasping at the cold touch of frozen fingers. They played there a while, kissing, tangled, hot, shutting out any thoughts of their inevitable end.

They both came noisily, gasping and trembling.

Manners chuckled, "Look at that, semen on a seaman."

Bottle rolled his eyes, but did quite like the view. Manners' pronounced muscles glistened, put on display by his open shirt, decorated liberally with pearls.

"Any regrets now?" Manners smirked.

Bottle shook his head.

*

Something rasped the outside of the hull. A slow, stroking motion, grating, grinding, scraping, moving from the torn midsection to the control room, and onward to the sonar dome at the front of the vessel. Bottle and Manners stiffened, listening, suddenly hyper-aware. They had fallen asleep in each other's arms, sticky and hot. Now they both shivered, and hurried to do up their trousers and shirts against the chill.

"What was that?" Bottle quivered.

"It sounded like something moving over the hull." Manners' chattering teeth made speaking a struggle.

The sound came again, this time moving across the ship rather than along it, changing direction and speed as it went. The sub rocked gently, shifting position upon whatever surface it had settled.

Bottle noticed the lights had dimmed considerably at the comms station. The back up battery was almost spent.

"There's something alive out there!" Manners hissed.

"Impossible." Bottle shook his head, "There's no life on Uranus."

"Well something is moving about out there, and it doesn't sound like a rescue craft, does it?" Manner's rubbed his hands together. He could only just see them in the dim light, and was sure they were blue.

Pulling his multi-tool out and taking it to the sonar controls with stiff, frozen fingers, Bottle shook his head, "They did surveys. There's nothing here."

"How do you know? That was hundreds of years ago. They might have missed something." Manners huffed tepid breath into his cupped hands.

With the facia removed, Bottle began to carefully manoeuvre his hands into the wires and mechanisms, searching with unfeeling fingers for the back-up battery buried within.

The sound came again, and as it moved over the stranded vessel, it rocked it violently. Both men fell onto their faces, rolling across the grated floor and into the far bank of controls. The noises stopped, and the submersible swung back the other way. It rocked back and forth slowly, settling again. As soon as he could safely stand, Bottle was back at the gizzards of the sonar controls, and up to his shoulders.

"If I can get a bit of power, I can get some idea of what's out there." He said.

Manners gripped a bulkhead for support, listening intently for the next attack. He was sure that's what it was, "It's Those Above. Come to finish us off."

"You're getting paranoid." Bottle said through gritted teeth, to keep them from chattering, "We must be getting low on oxygen. The recycling filters can't still be working."

With a loud bong the sonar controls sprang to life. Bottle pulled out his arms, and jammed the facia into place. He jabbed at buttons and twisted dials.

"Do you know what you're doing?" Manners asked urgently.

"Mostly. I've only started basic training on - ah!" He jumped back as a shower of sparks flew from some unseen exposed wire. They both stared at the green screens that hummed and binged and bonged before them. The echoes of the machine's various sounds began to build up a three-dimensional image of their surroundings. Pixel by flickering pixel, dot by faltering dot, the image expanded, zooming out from the silver line that represented the *Didsbury*.

The sea-bed seemed alive with wriggling, writhing arms. Long rubber-hose fronds, waving in the current. Those nearest the submarine seemed to be reaching for it, one at a time.

"What's that, over there?" Manners asked, pointing at a point nearby, where there appeared to be a depression in the seabed. As they watched, the depression changed shape; puckering, bulging, and then something shot out.

Bottle adjusted a dial to bring the focus back in close, and as the object moved over them, they gasped.

"It's the rear end of the sub!" Manners held his hands to his mouth in shock.

*

"A kind of anemone, or starfish, or something?" Manners suggested, stamping his feet to keep warm.

"Or something." Bottle nodded.

"And we're slowly being pushed towards its mouth?"

"Do they even have mouths?"

"I think they just have one suits-all-occasions multi-purpose hole." Manners grimaced.

Something crackled and spat static. It was the comms panel. Bottle rushed over and hefted the large headphones over his head. A faint signal was coming through. A series of beeps and blips. Morse code.

"What is it?" Manners asked.

Bottle sshhed him with a wave of his hand, straining to listen.

The bleeps and blips faded into static.

"It's one of our sister ships. Don't know which. They said 'SOS received, help is on the way'. Then they started to say something else, maybe 'signal'? I don't know."

The lights of the comms station died as the battery perished.

"Signal?" Manners muttered, "What do they mean?"

Bottle shook his head, "I'm not sure. Maybe they're struggling to find us? Maybe we need to send them a signal?"

"How? With no power, what can we do?"

Then Bottle had an idea.

*

"You're mad!" Manners said, pulling a woolly jumper over his head. Now that there was a glimmer of hope, he felt the need to wrap up against the cold. He pulled on a pair of thick welding gloves too, for good measure.

Bottle was struggling into a diving suit. The heavy boots and thick pressure-resistant fabric was top of the range equipment, and gleamed in the dim red light. It didn't look like it had ever been used.

"If they can't locate us, we need to send them a signal. An obvious signal."

"Can't we use the sonar for that?"

"It's muffled by the tentacles, or wherever they are around us. A sonar beam wouldn't make it far enough."

"You're mad." Manners repeated.

"It's the only way. It's ridiculous, but what other choice have we got? Now go and get those explosives like I asked?"

Manners nodded, and hurried away.

Bottle sighed, and crossed his fingers for luck.

*

Bottle moved slowly in the heavy suit, dragging his air supply tube behind him. He walked through a moving forest of tendrils. The arms of whatever creature they had landed on were lit by some gentle internal phosphorescence.

"It's like walking through a misty wood." He said into his comms link.

His bulbous metal helmet was fitted with round windows, allowing only narrow fields of vision to the front, sides, and above.

Manners had kissed him before the helmet had been screwed into place. He could still feel that kiss on his lips.

"Hurry up." Manners' urgent voice crackled back to him, "Please."

The going was made all the more laborious due to the equipment strapped to Bottle's back, and the length of cable that unwound from his hip, the end of which was tethered to several sturdy points along the side of what remained of the *Didsbury*. Which, as Bottle had noted, was less than he expected.

Step by step he drew closer to the depression in the seabed, the mouth, the cloaca, the whatever-the-hell-orifice that the arms encircled. The arms waved in unison, sweeping this way and that in the dense, liquid ice sea.

Eventually Bottle reached the edge of the clearing, and whistled through his teeth at the scale of the puckered hole that stretched out before him. He removed the heavy load from his back, and began attaching the contents to the reel of cable at his hip. Bombs, removed from their balloon floats, clustered together into bundles of ten. There were five bundles. There was also a series of weights; heavy pieces of metal, that Bottle attached to the cable with the explosives.

"I'm all set." Bottle said.

"Do it, and get back here pronto." Manners' voice crackled back.

Bottle released the cable from the side of the diving suit and attached it to the harpoon gun slung over his shoulder. He aimed it high, and fired. The harpoon launcher had just enough power to send the explosive parcels half way to the hole, where they rolled and tumbled slowly to a stop.

"Damn it." Bottle said.

"What?"

"The payload didn't go in."

"Shit."

Bottle stared at the packaged bombs and weights, their last desperate hope at salvation, and made a decision.

He strode forward, slowly, following the cable. The texture of the seabed changed beneath his boots.

It became spongy and sticky, slowing him down further. But he struggled on, and made it to the bombs. Carefully he picked them up, and carried them closer and closer to the centre of the clearing. He could see the muscles around the opening flexing. Were they reacting to his presence? The movement beneath his feet made him unsteady, and he stumbled, landing heavily on top of the explosives. They didn't go off. Sweating and grinding his teeth, Bottle stood up and continued on. When he reached what he deemed an adequate distance, he dropped the explosive package, and pushed it towards the opening. The flexing, puckering hole slurped the package down. Down, down down it went into the beast. The cable went taught, and he felt the sea bed gulp beneath his boots.

"Bon voyage, Manners." Bottle said into the comms unit as he pressed the detonator, and the bombs went off.

The creature's opening bulged and gaped, as an enormous ball of bubbling flames shot out. The weighted package of explosives was expelled by the creature, launching it in a graceful red-hot arc over the remains of the stricken *Didsbury*. The tendrils coiled in pain, and their glow flashed brightly, angrily.

Aboard the *Stockport*, someone said, "I have them, sir. Lowering the grappling arm for recovery."

The ascent was slow, so as to prevent the bends. Manners lay on his bunk for the whole journey, staring at the empty one below his.

There was a memorial service a week later, where seaman James Bottle was posthumously awarded several medals.

"What good will they do him?" Manners muttered to himself, as he watched Bottle's tearful mother collect the shiny trinkets on her son's behalf.

An investigation was launched, the results of which ended the war; so shocking was the result. Those Above came together with Those Below in a pledge to Do No Harm To Uranus.

"For this world on which we live, in whose waters we sail, is no mere ball of ice and rock." Said the commodore of Those Below at a grand ceremony, "Uranus is alive. It is an aware, feeling, thinking being, on whose back we have been as lice these past long years of conflict. But no more."

The commodore of Those Below shook hands with the commodore of Those Above, and politicians nodded sagely from the seats around them.

"This will now be known as James Bottle Day, a celebration of his life and the discovery that his sacrifice led us to. The dawning of a new age of peace and companionship. For all of us; Above, Below, and Uranus itself."

ALSO AVAILABLE
by Rylan John Cavell

in the AND OTHER STORIES range:
The Blood Moon (vol 1)
The Scarecrow's Lament (vol 2)

Novellas:
The PolGnomes and the Vile Grumble
The Analogue Archive

Novels:
Professor Calamity *books 1 & 2*
Violence & Lavender
Pity The Dead

Fambles Anthologies:
Good For Nibbles?
Year Of The Zoom!
Once Upon A Lockdown
The Novelty Has Worn Off
Menswear

www.rylanjohncavell.com

www.ingramcontent.com/pod-product-compliance
Lightning Source LLC
Chambersburg PA
CBHW061427160726

47995CB00003B/789